Photo by Steve Payne

HOWARD ENGEL won the 1990 Harbourfront Festival Prize for Canadian Literature and the 1984 Arthur Ellis Award for Crime Fiction. In 2005 he received the prestigious Matt Cohen Award in Celebration of a Writing Life. *Memory Book* is his first novel since the suffered a stroke in 2000, which him left with *alexia sine agraphia*.

OLIVER SACKS, MD, is a professor of clinical neurology at Albert Einstein College of Medicine. He is the author of many books, including *Awakenings* and *A Leg to Stand On*.

PRAISE FOR *MEMORY BOOK*

"The past tw   el,
one of the fe   ed
one of the m

                                                                      w)

"A slick mys

                                                                     ail

"Engel is a b   in
a few lines."

ell

DEMCO

Also by Howard Engel

The Suicide Murders

Murder on Location

Murder Sees the Light

A City Called July

A Victim Must Be Found

Dead and Buried

Murder in Montparnasse

There Was an Old Woman

Getting Away with Murder

Mr. Doyle & Dr. Bell

The Cooperman Variations

DATE DUE

HOWARD ENGEL

WITH AN AFTERWORD BY OLIVER SACKS, MD

CARROLL & GRAF PUBLISHERS

NEW YORK

MEMORY BOOK

Carroll & Graf Publishers
An Imprint of Avalon Publishing Group Inc.
245 West 17th Street
11th Floor
New York, NY 10011

AVALON
publishing group incorporated

Library of Congress Cataloging-in-Publication Data is available.

Publisher's note: This book is a work of fiction. Names, characters, places, and incidents either are the product of the author's imagination or are used fictitiously, and any resemblance to actual persons living or dead, events, or locales is entirely coincidental.

Simcoe College is a fictionalized college at the University of Toronto.

Cloth edition ISBN-13: 978-0-78671-644-9
Cloth edition ISBN-10: 0-7867-1644-4

Trade paperback edition ISBN-13: 978-0-78671-717-0
Trade paperback edition ISBN-10: 0-7867-1717-3

9 8 7 6 5 4 3 2 1

Printed in the United States of America
Distributed by Publishers Group West

This work is for
Cathy Nelson

MEMORY BOOK

THE DREAM

THE TRAIN WAS PUTTING ON SPEED. The wheels chattered, the pitch became higher. My fellow passengers didn't notice. Anna Abraham, sitting beside me, continued to read her book. Through the window and ahead of me, the tracks maintained a steady, level cut across the landscape. I could see a curve to the left, a tight curve. We were going into it too fast! The wheels were screaming. Nightmare sounds of metal on metal. The coaches were bending away from the tracks. Wheels were coming off the steel. I could feel the danger in my spine. We were going to turn over. Centrifugal or centripetal forces. I couldn't remember which. Maybe both.

The train lurched. Brakes screeched. Then an uncanny silence, like the silence of falling. I couldn't see Anna anywhere. We *were* turning over! Briefcases and luggage tumbled over me. I thought of the pictures in *Alice in Wonderland*. Coffee cups and playing cards flew around me and overhead. Paper money and change were momentarily suspended in mid-air as the bottom of the coach became the top. Newspapers and glossy magazines obscured the inverted landscape outside the window. A suitcase with metal-reinforced corners came floating toward me through the confusion of flying objects. I tried to avoid it, not too difficult a task since everything seemed to be moving in slow motion. But the heavy suitcase clipped me above my left eye, into blackness, and I went down in a tempest of flying objects.

ONE

IT IS A TRUTH UNIVERSALLY ACKNOWLEDGED that a private investigator who acts on his own behalf is an idiot who has a fool for a client. However true this may be, a circumstance occurred a year ago that may go a mile or two toward rehabilitating the fool. It all began when I opened my eyes on strange surroundings: white walls and suspended curtains. A face near mine spoke.

"What?" I yelled.

"I *said,* 'Do you know where you are?'" She was looking down at me, her face rather closer to mine than needed for normal conversation. And who was she, anyway?

"Do you know who I am?" Her hair smelled clean. Her face was close again. It came and went, like it was swinging on a string, or seen through a playful zoom lens. A horizontal yo-yo. It came closest when she talked, as though I might not understand her at a greater distance.

"No, I don't think so," I said. "But it seems like a good place to start. Who are you? You look familiar somehow."

I put that last part in to be polite. Part of it was nervousness. It's hard talking to strangers from a horizontal position. I was caught in an unfamiliar corner. This woman might be the key to something important.

"I'm Carol McKay, rhymes with 'day.' I'm a nurse here at the hospital. Do you remember that you are in the hospital?"

"I was on a train before. There was an accident. A train wreck."

"You weren't on a train, Mr Cooperman."

"Not a train?"

"Not a car either."

"Then why am I lying down? What sort of accident was it? Was I hit by a bus? A truck? What day is it?"

"You have no broken bones, Mr Cooperman. You haven't had a stroke or heart attack. And this is Friday, the twentieth."

"The twentieth! I've been here for most of the *month.*" I don't know where I got the notion that whatever put me in the hospital must have happened at the beginning of the month. It was just tidier for nasty things to happen at the beginning of the month. I was trying to be tidy. Confusion was the enemy. The nurse's brown eyes were fixed on me. I wet my lips and cleared my throat. "I haven't been in hospital since I had my tonsils out when I was a kid. The *twentieth*! April's nearly over!" I only had the vaguest notion of time. I don't know why I picked April. Maybe I was trying to show that I was still on top of things.

"April is over, Mr Cooperman. So is May. This is *June.* The twentieth." She glanced at the chart on the outside of her notebook. "You have been here for six weeks and you were at Mount Sinai for two weeks before that. You may not remember me, Mr Cooperman, but you've seen me before. In fact, we've had this same conversation before. But I'm not surprised you don't remember it. The brain has its own way of healing. We may have to go over it again tomorrow. It's all part of what we expect."

My being here had something to do with a train. Had I been on a trip? I couldn't remember. I'd forgotten the nurse's name, too. The pieces of the puzzle were slipping through my fingers.

Maybe I'd been drunk? No, I hadn't been drinking; it goes against my character, such as it is. This was getting more and more ridiculous. And why hadn't the news of all this brought me to my feet? When was the last time two weeks—*no, two months*—had vanished into limbo? Why wasn't I jumping up and down about it? And here I was, taking it in as though she'd been telling me what the menu was for lunch.

"I think I was in a train wreck."

"No, Mr Cooperman. No trains, cars, or buses."

I attempted to return her cool, even look, while trying to swallow at the same time. "Did I have a stroke or something? A heart attack? My father had a heart attack a few years ago. I know that my diet has not been the healthiest. Too many restaurant meals."

"Mr Cooperman ..."

"... I've tried to introduce more vegetables, less fat and ..."

"Mr Cooperman, you came to us from Brain Injuries at Mount Sinai Hospital. You had a trauma to your head."

Automatically, my hands explored the area on the upper left-hand side of my head, where it still felt tender. "How did I get this? Was I in an accident? Was I hit? Did I fall?"

"The injury is consistent with your having suffered a blow to your cranium."

"'Consistent with.' You sound like a lawyer."

"Looks like a blow to me. But I'm not a brain specialist; I've only been a nurse on this floor for twenty-two years. Nobody has suggested in my hearing that you did that falling. Looks to me as if you were hit from behind on the left-hand side." Somehow, I wasn't taking most of this in. It was as if she was telling me about somebody I hadn't met yet. I tried another tack.

"Do my mother and father know I'm here?"

"They've been in to see you almost every other day. They're staying with your brother. He's looked in on you, too, from time to time."

"*Sam* drove in from Toronto? Seventy-five miles? I'll bet!"

"But you're *in* Toronto. It's your *parents* who've had the long drive."

"Sorry. I'm still a bit thick in the head. Let's do the basics. I'll begin with the usual first question: Where am I?"

"Good beginning. This is the Rose of Sharon Rehabilitation Hospital on University Avenue in Toronto. This is the fifth floor and I'm Carol McKay, rhymes with 'day.' Next question?"

"How long have I been here?" I'd lost her name again. She consulted her clipboard.

"You were admitted to the hospital on April 11 and came to this ward two weeks later, the twenty-third of April."

"Will I ever walk again?"

"There's nothing wrong with your legs, Mr Cooperman. Don't you remember going to the bathroom?" As she said it, I seemed to remember the bathroom on the other side of the curtain. The curtain hung from tracks surrounding my bed. It seemed to me that I had dreamed of these tracks in the ceiling, but that memory was too scrambled to sort out. What's-her-name was looking at me.

"Are you all right?" she asked.

"What the hell is 'all right' in these circumstances? Will you tell me what's going on? Why can't I remember yesterday? What's wrong with me? What have I got to look forward to? Am I finished? That's the question, damn it."

"You don't want to raise your voice, Mr Cooperman. I can hear you. Don't get yourself excited. You are improving every day. Yesterday we didn't get nearly this far before you dozed off. Are you feeling tired now?"

"I want to know what's up first. How long will I be here?"

"That depends on your progress. Head injuries are slow healing; slower than fractures, slower than sprains, slower than most surgery. You're going to have to learn patience.

You're on the fifth floor. Everybody on five has had a stroke or brain injury. We'll see to it that you work with people who can help you get over the injury and others who will help you adjust."

"Damn it, I don't want to adjust! I have to be able to work. People depend on me. There are bills that need paying and things that can't be put off."

"I hear that all the time, Mr Cooperman, but patients learn that with a little time most things can be accomplished. Rome wasn't built overnight. We have to learn to walk before we learn to run. Just try to remain calm."

"Yeah, and walk directly to the nearest exit. We who are about to die salute you. Beautiful! This sounds like lifeboat drill on the *Titanic!*"

"It's early days, Mr Cooperman. Don't rush yourself into having a stroke. You may never again have such a good excuse for taking it easy. Are you getting tired?"

"No, damn it! I *told* you, I just want to know what's going on. You can't put me off with a bunch of platitudes. I know that day by day in every way I'm getting better and better. So, let's wave Pollyanna off into the sunset and get back to reality. Have there been any policemen looking for me?" How did I know the cops were involved? The nurse hadn't said anything. The idea came from me. Where did I get it?

Her eyebrows shot up. Good! At last I'd asked a question that made her expression change.

She took a moment to calm her features, then became the inquiring machine again. "The police have only asked if they will be able to speak to you when you feel better.

The police are not *after* you, Mr Cooperman. There's no guard at the door. They simply want to talk to you."

"Sure."

"Can you remember how you acquired this injury, Mr Cooperman?"

"A train fell on me. It turned over."

"You've said that before. Anything else?"

"I can't remember. If you know something, please tell me."

"You've had a serious blow to the back of your head. Can you remember anything about the time before the insult to your brain?"

"Insult? What happened was more than unpleasant words."

"It's our way of describing a serious brain injury, Mr Cooperman. It has nothing to do with bad manners," she said. "Now, can you think back to when you were little. Where was home?"

"Right here. The banks of the Eleven Mile Creek. My father runs a store."

"Good! Except that this is Toronto, not Grantham. What else can you remember?"

I turned my eyes back inside my head, figuratively speaking. I looked for anything that came to mind: images of children playing with alleys and marbles on the hard-packed earth of the schoolyard; the same children sliding down an icy slope behind Edith Cavell School; the principal, Mr Martin, whistling the end of recess through two fingers placed between his teeth.

"Public school's intact. I can remember the schoolyard and my grade six teacher."

"That's more than I can do. What about high school?"

I thought of the bus ride with wool-clad kids my own age. I could see the monumental façade of the collegiate, girls going up and down the stairs, carrying books before them, hugged to their young bosoms. I could see faces of my fellow students, lined up for an annual photograph, the teachers looking grave in serried ranks.

"Let's see. Mr Kramer (we called him Otto), Miss Smith, Mr Ogilvy, Mr James Palmer, Mr Price, Mr C. Evan Macdonald, Miss Smith ..."

"You said Miss Smith already."

"She was *worth* two mentions. They said she was a former cheerleader from the University of Toronto. That's what we wanted to believe, anyway." I recalled how we boys sighed for Miss Smith's history classes.

"What can you remember about last fall or this past winter? Were you working hard after the snow cleared? I'm sorry, Mr Cooperman, I'm a bit vague about what it is you do for a living. Are you a debt collector of some kind?"

"Sometimes it amounts to that. I'm a private investigator."

"Oh, like Sam Spade and Lew Archer?"

"Yeah, but without Bogart. I don't think he could have stomached the tedium."

"Can you remember any of your recent cases?"

I lay in silence thinking about this for some time before I could answer. "When I get close to the present, my memory is not as certain. Things, images, are more like Jell-O that hasn't set properly yet. I can picture my office and my apartment, but I can't quite remember where they are or how I get from the one to the other."

"Keep thinking about your work," she said.

I thought, trying to clear away the fog. All I could find were fragments, shards, confetti, like the pieces of a smashed dish. Echoes of voices in a great hall. Maybe a museum. Nothing that made sense. Then there was the recurring image of falling about in my tumbling railway car. Sometimes I could hear names from my past, forgotten names that I tried to place, to find a context for, to put a date on, to measure against some other familiar monument in my life. Doug Slack, Garth Dittrick, Billy Challace. Most of them I hadn't thought about in years. Kids from my kindergarten class, clients from my first cases, girls I'd dated only once, characters in novels and movies. The nurse was still waiting for an answer. I tried to remember the question.

"There were a couple of new cases." I was really rolling back the clouds now. I tried to picture the view from behind my desk. "I think there was a skipper, and ..." My mind wouldn't give up anything more. I tried harder until my head began to hurt. "Nurse, I know that loss of memory is called amnesia. It's a very popular device in old movies like *Lost Horizon* ..."

"That was the one about Shangri-La. You're thinking of *Random Harvest*. They're both from books by James Hilton. Are people still reading them?"

I was impressed, but not enough to let her off the hook. I was looking for the name of what afflicted me.

"Tell me about my amnesia," I said. "Is it temporary or permanent? How much of my memory is permanently blasted?"

"Well, Mr Cooperman, since you ask, I'll try to explain. As far as we can tell, your mind, your ability to think, to talk, to figure things out, is intact. Like the way you remembered the James Hilton novel just now. You picked the wrong title, but it was by the same author. That means that your cognitive powers are mostly intact. We have tested your reflexes and your motor abilities. All intact. You won't remember this, but last week you played chess with another patient. I think you won at least one game. That's the good news. The bad news is we are almost certain, from tests you won't remember now—"

"Tell me, damn it!"

"This isn't easy, Mr Cooperman. We think, we *know,* that you have lost much of your ability to read."

"To read!"

"That's right. You may not have noticed it yet, but we are more than pretty sure."

I looked around me blankly. I could see everything I could normally see. I saw the nurse, the curtains, the bump of my knees under the covers. Through the window, I could see the hospital across the street. There was nothing wrong with my vision. What's-Her-Name reached over to the folded newspaper by the window and handed it to me. I picked up the first section and opened it. I looked at it in disbelief. It could have been written in Serbo-Croatian or Portuguese or Greek. I couldn't make out the words. I squinted hard at the front page, recognizing the logo of *The Globe and Mail*. It was English, but the words below were foreign. My hands began to shake. Again I squinted hard; I could make out most of the letters—I saw *"The"* and *"and"*—but the normal black-and-white words kept their secrets from me. I couldn't decode the letters. I turned the page to see whether an inside page would yield a different story, a better result. It didn't. Not only was I an amnesiac, I was illiterate to boot! I must have blinked to stop the tears. That was all my damned eyes were good for.

I think I started to yell about then.

TWO

SOMEWHERE IN MY MIND I suspected a trick, a plot. I remembered an old movie in which the Nazis convince a captured Allied officer that he has just recovered from amnesia and that the war has been over for many years. To make the device work, they bleached his hair white, aged his face and skin, and showed him newspapers that had been specially concocted with a date well in the future that told of the Axis victory. They almost got away with it, until the officer remembered a recent paper cut on his finger that would have healed if so much time had passed. At the last moment, he was saved from giving away the Allied plans for the invasion of Europe. I resolved to look out for newspapers down the hall. The safest thing was to be suspicious of everything. For instance, if this was a real hospital, where were the doctors? I couldn't remember seeing any. I had them there!

"What's a skipper?"

"Huh?" It was my nurse, my own special nurse, whose name was ... I just noticed that she was black. From the

Caribbean, maybe. The fact wasn't important, but it hadn't registered earlier.

"You said you'd been working on a case involving a skipper."

"Oh, a *skipper*. A skipper is— Don't try to change the subject."

"We'll get back to the subject, I promise. Right now, you need a breather."

"A skipper's a deadbeat. This one was a poor guy from Grantham. I'd met him in an amateur theatre group a year before I had to deal with him professionally. Charming as hell. Small-time bunko artist, but a crook with the soul of a poet. He fell in love with the names of the legal firms that were prosecuting him! He loved the sound of their names: Trapnel, Fleming, Harris, Kerwin and Barr; Heatherington, Cavers, Goodwyn and Chown. He used to recite the names as if they were poetry. Not a bad fellow, really, not somebody you'd take to be a crook, but he lived high, never worked, and finally ran out on *both* the women he was exploiting. He claimed that alimony was bleeding him to death, which meant there had been other women. The one who hired me thought there was good in him that he hadn't discovered yet. She may be right: he once sent me a postcard from La Jolla, California. But right now I suspect he's down in New York State on a farm. His family comes from around there."

The nurse was rapt. I think that's the word for it. Entranced. I went on, "I once had another case of a deadbeat. This one got behind in his support payments to his wife and kids. Alimony. Accumulated arrears amounting to more than I make in a year." The nurse was right: talking about the past had a calming influence. I was amazed at myself. I'd just been told that I was cut off from the whole of the Grantham Public Library, to say nothing of the Grantham daily paper with my crossword in it, and I was chatting away as though my whole life hadn't just been flushed down the toilet. I paused, scanning my recent memory before going on. "I can't seem to remember my open files. I'll have to check the office as soon as I can drive down there."

"All in good time. What you have, Mr Cooperman, is called *alexia sine agraphia*. It's quite rare."

"What are the chances they'll name it after me?"

"There are better ways to be remembered."

"When you told me about my reading, I sort of blew up. I'm sorry about that. But did I let you finish? Is there more?"

"Are you ready for it? It's not as bad as not being able to read, but it's just as annoying."

"Better tell me. I'll be brave."

"You may have noticed this already. You forget things. You mix things up, like apples and pears, oranges and lemons. You remember faces better than you do names. Like mine, for instance."

"I'll get it yet. It sounds like something. Right?"

"Right. Carol McKay, rhymes with 'day.'"

I repeated the name under my breath, trying to anchor it in my brain. I didn't test it; I just held on to the hope.

She was looking down at me again with those playful brown eyes. "Have you been able to trace the edge, the time when your memory breaks off?"

"When I try too hard, everything implodes. I can't remember your name or even my own when I get rattled. It's better when it just comes to me. When I go after it, it's like trying to place a name at a crowded party. You have to winkle out a memory like that. No good galumphing after it. Hey, how is it that I can still talk and remember words like 'winkle' and 'galumphing'?"

"Has to do with the location of the blow to your head. An inch higher or lower and you might have trouble with other things. There was a case last Friday of a man who had lost the ability to swallow. That required surgery. Whoever hit you, Mr Cooperman, picked a good spot. With some time doing rehab, you'll be surprised by what you can do."

"Thanks," I said, without putting much life into it. I didn't want to make progress, I wanted to get on with my life. Anything less was makeshift and unsatisfactory. I could feel a deep depression beginning to percolate through my legs and into my stomach. A black mood had hove to in the harbour of my mind, awaiting further orders. Rehab, she'd called it. I could tell that I wasn't going to like rehab. Even before I started on it, it already had the aftertaste of artificial sweeteners.

"I know it's not what you want to hear, Mr Cooperman, but it's what we have to offer. If you walk down the hall, you'll see people worse off than you."

I didn't give a damn about the people down the hall. I wanted to roll over and face the curtain. She wasn't even going to allow me a moment of self-pity. If I couldn't feel sorry for myself now, when could I?

THREE

"YOU MUST TELL ME more about this Alex Graphic, or whatever it's called. Please, Rhymes With." We were still in my room. Or, maybe, we were here again and time had slipped by. The sun was lower, the lighting in the room was different.

"The term is *alexia sine agraphia*. It's Latin. Alexia is the inability to read because of a brain injury. You know that."

"What about the rest of it? *Sine* means without. I remember that much high-school Latin."

"Without *agraphia:* without *not* being able to write."

"Too many negatives. Does that mean I *can* or I *can't* write?"

"You can still write normally. I did tell you that it was a rare condition."

"What the hell use is it to be able to write if I can't read what I've written?"

"We didn't make up the rules to afflict you, Mr Cooperman. The act of reading and that of writing are not identical functions. Often when people lose one, they lose the other. But not in your case." Rhymes With was speaking just above a whisper. She wasn't finding this easy and I wasn't making it any easier for her.

I suppose it should have felt like she had given me half my life back again, but it didn't. Reading was Shakespeare and Hawthorne, Whitman and Poe. Not to mention Hammett, Chandler, and Macdonald, or Christie, Rendell, and James. Writing was only me. Not much competition there. I promised Rhymes With that we would have another chat later on. I could see that she was relieved to get away.

It was a sunny room. I couldn't complain about that. The suspended white curtains diffused the light coming from the windows so that both beds in the room got an equal share. The curtains even gave the impression of a breeze, of summer outings and tents pitched above a trout stream. This impression was muted by the panel of electrical outlets and receptacles for jacks and hoses above the beds. There was a bathroom somewhere and cupboards. The door to the hall was always open. The corridor beyond was usually lively with sounds of rubber-soled shoes and the tires of wheelchairs and gurneys.

Visits from the doctors were rare, and we made much of them. Doctors were the celebrities of the corridor. You could hear them coming. You could hear their voices as they made their way from room to room. The musical chatter of the nursing station was muted when the spoor of physician was in the air. When they were on the floor, theirs was the only buzz. Even the elevators' pinging seemed to stop. The doctors moved from bed to bed in a tight military formation. Every patient was given a dole of cheer before the phalanx moved on and the normal sounds of the day returned.

When dinner came on its rattling tray that night, I could still remember the morning's conversation with my nurse. Her news still had me reeling. I kept checking the accuracy of what she said against every scrap of paper at my command. If this was some kind of plot, it was a devilishly thorough one: not a scrap of printed paper contained printed words I could decipher. From *The Globe and Mail* to *Time* magazine. Maybe I should check out the books and papers in some of the other rooms. I'd thought of that in the morning, but had done nothing about it. I seemed to be suffering from a wounded initiative as well as what that scrap of Latin indicated. At the same time, I didn't feel so physically weak any more.

Dinner was roast mutton with gravy. The taste was fine, although I wondered whether the meat and the gravy had ever met before coming together on my plate. When I caught a glimpse of Rhymes With as she hurried down the central corridor, I was mildly irritated to see that she had a life quite separate and distinct from looking after me. I thought over what she had told me. I knew that she was a resource person and that I'd be foolish not to listen to her. I was also wondering where my depression had gone. I'd felt it brewing earlier, but it hadn't grown any bigger than a shy belch that wouldn't come out. I used to be able to brew a better storm than that over an empty cigarette pack. That was back in my smoking days. Now I could get into a panic about faulty mechanical pencils and conversations about computers.

I ate my meal with my legs over the side of my bed. Feet on the ground. That's me: Cooperman with his game well in hand, ready to rediscover the world.

This wasn't the full extent of my efforts. First, I discovered the curtain, suspended beside my bed, masked the fact that I wasn't alone in this room. I had a roommate. True, I had been aware in the distant marches of my consciousness that there were sounds coming from behind the curtain. Snores, mostly, and occasionally the buzz of visitors. He grinned at me once, but didn't speak. Same thing the next time.

I got up and went to the bathroom—a two-piece unit of heavy-duty porcelain. At first I thought it included a tub, but that must have been in some earlier room: there was no place to hide one here. There were printed signs attached to the wall to instruct patients in the use of the equipment: the correct form for flushing, I suppose, or the proper way to dispose of used paper towels. Not being able to read the words, I flushed the old-fashioned way without attracting attention.

Someone had unpacked my toiletries. They stood on display for the approval of my roommate, the cleaners, and nursing staff. I examined what was there. Did I stand here yesterday? Was I just as bewildered the day before? I picked up one bottle after another without recognizing the proper use of any of them. Was this toothpaste or shaving cream? Was this mouthwash, aftershave, or hair tonic? Smelling the contents helped solve the mysteries, but I know that at least once I cleaned my teeth with hair gel. I was bewildered by my bewilderment. I was next door to helpless. I couldn't read "PUSH" on a revolving door. After feeling braced a few minutes earlier, I now felt beaten, and went back to bed.

"W-w-w-what did you think of the … the … the stuff that they put on the meat, Benny?" It was my roommate.

"The gravy?"

"Yeah, the … *gravy*."

"It seemed innocent enough. Didn't you like it?" I got out of bed and pulled back the curtain between us.

"It … it … it was self-elf … effacing. Tried to keep its … its orig … orig … origins a secret. The meat was lamb, I think, but the … the …"

"Gravy."

"The g-g-gravy could have come from anything: old suitcases, discarded wallets, road-k-k-k-kill."

"It didn't seem so bad."

"Ah! Spoken like a … a … newcomer! You'll change your t-t-tune when you're closer to graduation."

My roommate was tall and skinny lying down. I didn't recall seeing him standing. A wheelchair was parked next to his bed. Maybe that was the reason. His greying hair was short-cropped, which gave him a military bearing. He managed to look dapper in his hospital gown, a trick I never learned.

"How long have you been here?" I asked.

"About s-s-s-sixt-t-teen weeks. Valentine's Day. I'm n-n-near the end. I'll be back f-f-f-for out-patient help l-l-later. They've got a separate s-section for that." He took a bite from a cookie and offered me one. "You've got a nice ... nice ... family. They come a-a-almost every ... every ... d-d-*day*."

"I don't remember." I took a cookie and nibbled on it.

"Y-y-your father, M-M-Manny, p-p-p-plays cards w-w-with me. Sophie brought me candy. Nice p-p-p-people."

"Yeah. I guess I'll have to learn to appreciate them better." I didn't understand the cynical tone in my voice. Maybe I thought that they should have stood between me and the accident. What did they have to do with it? Cooperman, get real!

"Did you f-f-f-finish your cookies at lunch?"

"Which ones were they?"

"Woolly. Th-th-that's the coconut. Blast it, how is it I can say 'coconut' b-b-but not simple words?"

"Don't sweat it. I can understand you fine. We're both in the same boat. I can't *read* but I can *write*. I'm going to mix up oranges and apples too. That's what they tell me. Not that I've seen much fresh fruit in here. The thing I can't understand is that both of us are taking it all so calmly. Why aren't we banging on the walls and sending out an SOS?"

"I th-th-think we've blown the p-p-p-p-protest valve too. M-m-m-makes for peace and qui-qui-qui-quiet."

"Is it something put in the food?"

"No, it's … j–j–just our wire–wire–wiring, Benny."

My neighbour had a laptop computer cradled in his lap, the first I'd ever seen in a real lap. I tried to remember my earlier conversations with him, but couldn't. He knew my name and seemed to be on a first-name basis with both my parents. I asked him, but he didn't remember what day I'd been put into this room or if I had said anything odd in my sleep.

"Y–y–you s–s–sleep most of the d–d–day," he said with a trace of envy. "Like a m–mole."

His eyes had a baleful look, which I cured, turning the frown to a grin, by carrying the rest of my dessert cookies across the space between us. He thanked me and set to the business of serious munching.

Walking back to my bed, I tried telling my brain to find any scrap of what had happened to me since I was admitted. There was nothing there. At the same time, this room and the people in the corridors all seemed familiar enough. I could accept that I had been here for some time. I didn't feel like a newcomer. I vaguely knew what lay beyond the turn in the corridors at both ends of the floor.

When I'd climbed back into bed, I wondered why I bothered. I wasn't sick. I didn't have a fever. I wasn't out of my mind. Then I got it: bed is a handy place to file people until you know what you want to do with them. In my pyjamas I was unlikely to get into the elevator, head out the front door and into traffic.

From my window, I could see the busy street, divided down the middle by a running island of flowerbeds and monuments to public figures. University Avenue, Toronto, Ontario, Canada. Still, every time I looked out the window, I expected to see Grantham's Queenston Street. My body was in Toronto, but half of my mind was at home in Grantham.

Across the street and up a bit, I could see the brick-and-cement shell of a hospital wing that was being demolished. Was it my imagination that informed me that the ruin had been taller earlier in the week, or was it just a safe inference? There wasn't a lot I knew for sure. The old wing—bricks, mortar, and the steel frame still partly covered in cement—was solid while it lasted. Until both of us dissolved into a new stage of falling apart, we appeared stable enough. The feet I used to walk my cookies across to my roommate were recognizably my own feet. Maybe a little greyer or bluer than I remembered them—I blame that on my poor circulation after being flat on my back for all this time—but they were indisputably my own feet. The thoughts in my head also sounded like my own familiar voice. If the mind was my own, then all wasn't lost.

I looked at my belongings stretched out on a low table to the right side of my bed, under the window. I recognized most of them, but others I had to pick up and handle before finding some past echo attac\hing them to me. A portable radio was out of place lying next to a familiar pair of sunglasses. The glasses were mine; the radio wasn't. Both facts I could deal with. I sat on the edge of my bed for a few minutes, wondering why it was that I got up and put my feet on the cold floor with such dispatch. After a few minutes thinking about it without success, I tried not thinking about it, with better luck.

Then, it hit me: if I had a brain injury and it wasn't caused by a stroke, then it must have been a blow of some sort, a rap on the head. Was it that train I'd been dreaming about? What hit me? I looked around to see if Rhymes With was within hailing distance. No. I knew that I'd better calm myself or I'd go off the deep end again. I needed calmer thoughts. Think calm thoughts.

I remembered that the names of all the patients were printed in large letters outside our rooms. I slid into my slippers and examined the printed names from the hallway. It took only a moment or two to recognize and eliminate my own name, then I painfully sounded out the letters on the other sign: "*Fos*, no *Suc, Suc-hard*, no, the *c* and the *h* go together." It took me a few minutes to decipher it, solving one letter after another. It wasn't speed-reading, but it was a beginning. My roommate's name was Jerry Suchard. By the time I had walked down the hall to the nursing station and back, refreshed my memory by looking at the name on the wall again, and then climbed back into bed, I could remember only the first name. I remembered struggling several times to recall my nurse's name. I had to face it: names were going to be a continuing problem. I tried scribbling Jerry's name on a scrap of paper so it would be handy when I needed it. My inventiveness impressed me, even when the *aide-mémoire* took me three minutes to decipher.

I had always had a horror of forgetting names. At the same time, I was always doing it. I could think of dozens of occasions where memory had failed in the middle of an introduction.

Now, of course, it wasn't a matter of not remembering one name in a crowd. Now I could no longer remember *any* name. I was going to live in a world where friends, colleagues, and relatives looked their familiar selves, but their names were all crowded into the lock-up at the end of my tongue. An oubliette, in more ways than one.

The funny thing was that I wasn't panicked. I didn't rejoice and embrace it, naturally, but I wasn't broken in half by it either. I'd get on; I'd manage. I'd never been heavy on the vocative before I got hit on the head. Now I had a good excuse, one that didn't put a dunce cap on my pointed head anyway.

Maybe I dozed off for a while. When I was myself again, my roomie had company. She had a thick Hungarian accent; he called her by a name I'd never heard before. Listening in shamelessly, I learned that she had just returned from Europe, where air travel had been upset for days because of some political crisis that seemed to excite both of them. I made a mental note to try to find out what the trouble in the old country was, not that my mental notes were worth anything; my mind was made of Swiss cheese.

"Dagmar," that was her name. I drifted off to sleep again into a dream of my train wreck punctuated with distant echoing voices repeating "Dagmar" and "Jerry." Then I remembered that a question had been nagging me. Something about the bang on my head. But what was it?

FOUR

"HOW ARE YOU HOLDING UP, BENNY?" My eyes were closed; I was just starting the cycle that led to the train wreck. It wasn't Dagmar or my roommate, Jerry. It was Sam, my brother. I still couldn't get used to the idea that my dear brother would come all the way to Grantham to see me. Maybe he knew something about my condition the nurse hadn't told me.

"*Damn,* it's good to see you, Sam. You're a doctor, give me the lowdown on this thing. And don't spare my feelings."

"Sure, Benny, as you like it. You were hit on the back of the head with a blunt instrument about eight weeks ago. You started waking up only just this week. We thought we'd lost you a couple of times, but you held on. Technically, you've got a fractured skull. There was some displacement, but it'll never show now we've fixed it, unless you lose all your hair. The people here on this floor are going to help you while you're still an in-patient, and then, for a while, after you've been discharged. They're going to work on your problem areas and get you the best help available."

"What are my problem areas, Sam? I seem to be able to walk and talk. I can still cut my meat and remember who I am."

Sam, my dear older brother, was looking down at me over his half-moon glasses. His hair was showing grey around the ears and his suit dealt with his middle-age paunch effectively. There were laugh lines at the corners of his eyes. He looked comfortable and happy. I took courage from that.

"Look, Benny, you've been very lucky. Lots of people up here are much worse off than you."

"Damn it, Sam! I'm not trying to win a disability contest."

"When they found you, you were in very bad shape. You'd lost a lot of blood from your head wound. Not from the brain itself. But the scalp and tissue around the area made it look as though you'd been shot in the head. You understand? Dr Collins says that your immediate memory is in a shambles and that you're going to have some difficulty reading. You can write, but you can't read what you've written."

"Sounds like a case for that American doctor, the one who wrote *The Man Who Mistook His Wife for His Hat*."

"Oliver Sacks? This would be right up his alley. But before we sell your story to the movies, let's get you back on your feet and functioning as well as we can."

"Great!" I said through my teeth.

"Sacks, by the way, is English. I'll see if I still have his latest book in my office."

"It's a picture book?"

"Sorry, Benny. I forgot. Maybe it's available on tape."

"Okay, I'll stop dreaming of TV contracts. How long am I going to be in here?"

"Don't be in such a rush to get out. Rod Collins knows what he's doing. I've talked to him. He's going to send you for tests ..."

"What kind of tests?"

"Don't be so suspicious, Benny. They want to map your visual fields, to see what damage has been done. That will help when you apply to get your driver's licence back."

"My licence was in my wallet."

"It's been suspended."

"What?"

"Now don't bend yourself out of shape about this, Benny. They suspend the licence of anyone who's had a serious brain injury. You're not special."

"They didn't take away that actor's licence! In Los Angeles. I read it in the paper just last month."

"Last month? Last month you were still in a *coma.*"

"Well. Whenever it was. Before I learned not to read. I saw a piece about What's-his-name, the movie actor. He got his licence back!"

"Ontario isn't California and you aren't Douglas Kirk. Doug Kirk had a different sort of injury. He had a stroke, for one thing. The effects are similar, I grant you, but not identical. Different strokes hit different folks. That's why they are not trying a one-size-fits-all approach. It's not the Hollywood lobby ganging up on a poor Canadian private eye. Frankly, I think you got the better deal."

"Thanks, and while I'm at it, thanks for driving out to see me so often. The nurse told me. I appreciate it, Sam."

"Drive? I don't under— Oh, Benny! You think you're still in Grantham!"

"Well?"

"Benny, you are in Toronto. This is the hospital where I work. Remember the Rose of Sharon? You did some work for me here last year."

"The Rose of...? Not Grantham General?"

"Right! It's Mom and Dad who have been coming in from Grantham to see you every few days. I'm putting them up at my place. My kids have never had a visit with their grandparents like this before. We're in your debt, Benny."

"Did I know about this?"

"About what?"

"Coming from Grantham to Toronto?"

"Benny, we just want what's best for you! We brought you to the best place for what ails you. You needed—"

"*Forget about that!* I'm just trying to find out where I am, when I got to Toronto, and whether I was here when I got hurt. Where did I get hurt? Here or at home? What can you tell me?"

"Benny, brother dearest, you lost me."

"Sorry I jumped at you, Sam. It's just that I get confused. I've been looking down at University Avenue all day. I *know* it's Toronto. How is it that in another part of my head I think I'm in Grantham? Can I carry two mutually contradictory notions in my head at the same time?"

"You'll get through the confusion. You received your injury here in Toronto. According to the police report, you were pulled out of a Dumpster."

"A Dumpster?"

"That's right, a Dumpster. One of those large garbage-collector things. In the middle of Toronto. Do you remember that part?"

I nodded, just to keep him going. I asked him whether he had known that I was in town, whether we had seen one another before the accident. He said that the first he heard about it was when he got a call from the cops.

"The Dumpster was on the property of a building on Spadina Avenue, where the university owns and operates a residence for fourth-year students and graduate students. Under the O that hangs over the street. Clarendon House. I'll show you the spot. Don't worry."

"Had I been in touch with you, Sam? I mean, was I staying at your house?"

"No. Nobody at the house had heard from you. I figure that you must have just arrived in town, since you usually stay with us."

That wasn't always true, but Sam didn't need to know that. He was faster than I was at figuring out that I must have just driven in from Grantham, where I still live and where Sam and I were brought up. The truth of the matter was that there have been times when I've been in Toronto and have chosen, for one reason or another, not to contact Sam and stay with him. Even my damaged pate could see the delicacy of not exploring this line further with my brother.

For some reason, Sam was making me nervous. I couldn't put my finger on the problem. But then, I had never looked down at *my* brother in a hospital bed. How long did he say I had been in a coma?

"Sam, I want to know all about what happened. You seem to be rationing the information. Tell me about the accident. Did my car run into the Dumpster?"

"Benny, there was no accident. Your car wasn't involved. It wasn't a traffic accident of any kind, not a hit and run."

"So, it wasn't random, not an accident?"

"That's right."

I caught my breath and looked at the remaining possibilities. "Then it was some kind of assault?"

"That's what we think. It wasn't robbery; your wallet was still in your pocket with sixty-seven dollars in it."

"Who lives in that residence? Anybody I know?"

"Mostly grad students with a handful of senior undergrads. The residence is at the corner of Spadina and Wessex, just north of Harbord."

"Place with the big letter O hanging over the street?"

"That's the place."

I remembered seeing it before, while it was being built. In fact, it became one of the sights I counted on seeing when I came to Toronto, like the CN Tower and the SkyDome. I could never be sure whether the giant letter was a design feature or a temporary part of the construction process. But it was still there when the scaffolding came down and the students moved in. Now the O appeared as the last letter in the word "Toronto." Soon it was dripping icicle meltwater over the intersection.

"I know that the cops have been taking an interest in what happened."

"How do you know that, Benny?"

I paused for about ten seconds. "I don't know how I know that. Maybe it was one of the nurses."

"They weren't supposed to tell you."

"What do you mean, not tell me? Who declared a news blackout? Sam, you know I don't like being manipulated."

"Settle down. Don't lose your cool."

"I *always* lose my cool when I've got a cracked skull."

"Don't have a stroke on me. Calm down."

"Do you know which cops are taking the biggest interest?"

"No, I don't. They'll be in touch when you are feeling stronger. Meanwhile, what do you need?" At this point, the conversation grew domestic. We discussed razors and underpants with a seriousness that was new to both of us. Sam jotted down my suggestions on the back of an envelope and in about ten minutes was saying his goodbyes.

So, I was working or visiting in Toronto when I got hurt. I hadn't a clue why I had been in Toronto, nor why I was a hundred kilometres from my office, where the mystery could be cleared up. My records might not satisfy the more scientific of my colleagues, but I'd always been able to give a fair account of my activities both in court and to the tax people. I always kept track of my cases and where my money came from. If I was in Toronto on business, then there had to be some record of it. It was a two-hour drive from Toronto in the middle of the afternoon. Then I remembered that my driver's licence was suspended. Damn it! I was further away than ever from getting to the bottom of this.

I tried to find a piece of paper and something to write with. I found the stub of what might have been an eyebrow pencil or a failed crayon and tried to use that to make a note on the fly-leaf of a book some predecessor had left behind.

If I had *driven* from home to Toronto in my own car, then certain things had to follow: after this length of time, my Olds must be somewhere collecting parking tickets or beginning to attract attention of some kind. Locating the car was a first step in tracing my reason for being in Toronto. There might be an address, a note, a name. Something. I made a note on the fly-leaf of the old book, again surprising myself that I still remembered how to make my letters. I took my eyes off what I'd written, looked out the window for a moment, then tried to read my writing. I got the first letter wrong, tried again, working out the relationship between the letters that made them into words. When I got about halfway, I remembered how the rest of it went. I sighed, then closed the book.

The book was *The Lady in the Morgue* by Jonathan Latimer, as I discovered after three minutes of hard work breaking the code of the letters. I flipped to the title page. It had been written before I was born. But it had real staying power in the hospital library. I remembered the author's name. It was buried in the farthest colonies of my memory. An aunt, who was always reading, had told me about him. The author had got himself in trouble with Senator Joseph McCarthy's House Un-American Activities Committee during the 1950s. Why did I remember things like that when I still couldn't get my nurse's name straight?

I fished my wallet from my clothes, which were stuffed into the small closet near the bathroom. I was tired. Being kept in bed steals all kinds of resources. Strength tops the list.

Pulling my cards and papers from my wallet was a peculiar exercise, like pulling out the wallet of someone who could no longer do the job for himself. The wallet itself could have belonged to a stranger. There were no clues that announced, "Hey! Remember when you tore this bit of leather? Remember this photograph of Ma and Pa?" The photographs did reassure me, but the feeling that I was going through the papers of "the deceased" lingered. And at the back of my mind there remained the half-formed question: how did these pictures get here? It was as though the contents of my wallet existed independently, without reference to anything I had done. Then there were pictures of people I didn't recognize, as well as others of faces that were familiar, but whose names had fallen off the table of my memory.

Once I was back sitting on my bed, facing the window, I pulled the phone toward me. I punched in the familiar number of the Motor Vehicle Registry. Of course, it was the *Grantham* number, so I hung up. I felt like I was handling the phone wearing boxing gloves. I tried to find the phone book: nowhere in sight. I dialled information, and told the mechanical voice that I wanted to reach Motor Vehicles: Lost or Stolen, at Toronto Metropolitan Police. An operator came on the line and told me that there was no longer any such municipality. She referred me to the Bell directory. I swore that there wasn't one in sight. She asked me a couple of questions about the nature of my business and which part of the city I was calling from. Soon, I became flustered and ended the conversation by hanging up. I'd become confused between answering her questions based on where I was now and trying to guess where the car might have been when it went missing. I could smell the sweat on the back of my neck. I couldn't understand this; I wasn't facing down a gunman, I was trying to get through to a police department to find out whether or not my car had been towed into the police garage or to the local pound. As I hung up, I was shaking, overcome by a wave of inertia. Suddenly, telephone operators had become as unfriendly as the Gestapo. Obviously, I had a long way to go in trying to figure out how to work around this brain injury of mine.

FIVE

DR RON COLLINS CAME BY the next morning accompanied by
three interns and an equal number of nurses. They came
in a tight formation, like a phalanx of warriors, shoulder
to shoulder. The doctor addressed me directly in a friendly,
bantering tone; he had another voice for his submissive
entourage.

"So, *you're* Cooperman's brother, are you? (Harper,
have a good look round the back.) He's a good fellow.
Plays a terrible game of golf. (The fracture's coming along
nicely. No displacement, you see, Harper.) Glad to see
you getting on. (Let someone else see, Garbett.) Lift your
right arm, Mr Cooperman. (He was comatose for seven
weeks.) Now your right leg. Touch the tip of your nose,
Mr Cooperman, with the middle finger of your right
hand. Very good! Left hand. Thank you very much." It was
quite a performance; he could patronize Sam and me
while entertaining his captive audience.

The three nurses now stood a degree removed from

the interns, leaving a deferential neutral space between them. Were these the remnants of ancient battle lines? The doctor talked on, not noticing. "Mr Cooperman, here, has a classic case of alexia without the often attendant agraphia. Mr Cooperman will sit up for us now, so we may examine the back of his head. Kindly slip out of bed, Mr C, so we can get a squint at you ..."

He went on to enlighten the interns, but without passing anything new along to me. It was a theatrical display, lacking only the rattle of a snare drum to keep the tempo brisk.

"Apart from your difficulty reading, are there any other visual problems?"

"Not really. I— Oh! I was looking at the rain coming down the window one day. It was dripping down the window in vertical lines. When I looked at it, the picture began breaking up, like a bad TV reception. The picture divided into narrow vertical slices, like a Venetian blind, but up and down, not across."

"Uh-huh. You tell me if you see that again."

"Another thing: whenever I see circles, they seem to get bent out of shape: like bicycle wheels that have been in an accident."

"Well, well, well, gentlemen, we have symptoms abounding. You will keep us abreast of any new developments, won't you, Mr Cooperman?"

The doctor was a dapper little man with tailoring that translated into big bucks, if you could read the messages. Still, he had nicked his chin shaving this morning; so everything wasn't rosy in his life. His thinning hair was combed artfully across his pink scalp. The interns and nurses remained suspended by his machine-gun-like comments on everything from my blood pressure to the blinking fluorescent tube behind my bed.

"This shouldn't put you off your golf game for long, Mr Cooperman. You'll be back on the course in a few weeks. Good morning. I'll look in on you again later in the week."

After they'd gone, it took me a few minutes to recover my identity. I did better when I wasn't being examined under a microscope.

I lay back in my bed thinking. I had a lot to think about.

Yesterday—I thought it was yesterday—I could never be sure any more—I thought I could pick up the pieces of whatever investigation I was working on and start making up for lost time. Now I realized that before I could get back on the trail, I had to throw away still more time recovering.

So, recognizing that I could see myself getting a little obsessive around the ears, I decided to ease off on the desire for fast and dispassionate revenge on whoever had put me in hospital. I would even agree to give up the dispassionate part. A good old-fashioned revenge would suit me fine.

Although I wanted to get on with my life, I could see that I was still not in any shape to deal with a snippy telephone operator, let alone the villain who clobbered me. Back off, Cooperman! Catch your breath.

Chandler says that a detective has to do his job no matter what. He could have said, "A man's gotta do what a man's gotta do." I could see that logic working in books and in the movies, but in real life it's tougher. What brought me here? I went too far, I guess; I got too close. I'd upset my attacker enough for him to take extreme measures. Hell, I was lucky he didn't do a better job on me.

Of course, when my memory cleared, when I was back on my feet, that would be a different proposition. I could see that; detectives in books have to have a narrower code of honour. There's no time for PIs in books or movies to lie about, recovering. The story has to move. To gallop! The fictional detective has an audience following his every move. He's never alone. He always has to do the right thing. He's like that salesman in the play I saw in summer stock: he's only got a smile and a shoeshine working for him. If this was a movie, I'd crawl out of my hospital bed, shake my head under the shower, and tear off the bandages as I grabbed my clothes on my way back to the street. The camera wouldn't miss a thing.

How many of my old cases would make good movies? Not many. The people with the problems weren't important enough. The villains, too were, nobodies. When there was a swindle, the money or property involved wouldn't have excited a real New York–based bad guy. A scam artist from LA wouldn't get excited about my best cases. And for an Englishman, my cases have been too random, not confined to a tidy manor house with a suspicious butler and a library full of suspects at the end. Now, how did my mind take me here?

I picked up the novel beside me. The letters swam meaninglessly into one another. Groups of two or three letters caught my eye with a distant familiarity, like a half-remembered face in a crowd. "The," I read. "The lady ... in ..." I kept on with it: *"The Lady in the Morgue."* The word "morgue" gave me a hard time, but I managed to decipher it: *"The Lady in the Morgue* by Jonathan Latimer." Had I known that? Had I already read this? I'd leave my problem to someone like Jonathan Latimer's two-fisted, ironic private eye, William Crane. Do it for me, Bill. Attaboy!

"What are you grinning at?"

I knew the voice. I turned and saw Anna. I nearly leaped out of bed, but she closed the distance between us faster than I could direct the thought to my legs. It was a clinch right out of the movies. Later, crediting Byron, Anna told me that the only proper measure of a kiss was its length. I agreed; the poet knew more about kissing than many pre-Victorians.

"Well!" she said, as we began to catch our breath, "you seem thoroughly restored in some departments. How does your head feel?" She was sitting on the edge of my bed. The look of concern on her face was serious.

"I'm fine," I said. "I don't even think about my head. It's my memory and things *inside* my head that are giving me trouble. It's like trying to find my way in a house of mirrors. I'll have to learn how to use the distortions to point the way to the truth."

"Always the philosopher! Candide reborn! Still digging in the manure pile hoping to find a pony down there."

"Not even imaginary ponies live in dung heaps. I've missed you, professor."

"Me too. Are they treating you right?"

"I'm fine. I get to argue with my nurses, and soon I'll be having my meals with the others down the hall. I'm in terrific shape, really."

"Do you remember my earlier visits? The nurses said you probably wouldn't."

"I remembered your *name,* didn't I? Don't be greedy. But the nurses are right; I don't remember anything earlier than today. Or yesterday. Recently. I'll remember this visit."

"Promises, promises."

"What do you know about what happened? I hope you're not part of this conspiracy to keep me guessing."

"Look, Benny, I just popped in to say hello. I'm late and illegally parked. Don't make me any later than I am already. To give fair answers to those questions, I'll need more time than I have right now. But don't despair. I'll be back in two days. Okay?"

"Sure."

"No, don't mope. Anyway, I see that I'm being ousted by a nurse with a bar of soap and a sponge. And right now you need a wash and brush-up more than you need the little I can add to what you know already. I'll try to call you tonight."

In a moment she'd been replaced by a strange nurse who went all over me with rubbing alcohol or something, chattering away my fragile memories of Anna's short visit. I let the rub-down pull me away from my anger and frustration into a somnolent feeling of dissolving tensions and my current default position: sleep.

The lights were on when I looked up again. The days passed quickly in the hospital. My roommate was snoring softly on the other side of the room, but the sky was still bright enough to be called day. Somewhere, out of my ken, the sun was sinking, leaving a rosy stain that marked the brickwork on the walls and rooftops of the hospital across the street. I took a look at the novel in my hand. Opening it at random, I tried to read the words. The first word looked like "posting." I went on to the next: "uncertainly." Posting uncertainly? Didn't make sense. Must be "pausing uncertainly." Yeah, that was better. I went on, decoding the words and word combinations one at a time, and returning to the beginning of the sentence to make sure I hadn't lost the sense. "Pausing uncertainly on the goddamn step." Something not right; look again. Sharpening my focus, "goddamn" became "gotton," then "bottom." Yes! Bottom! "On the bottom step …" And so it went, phrase by phrase, line by line, until I was too tired to go on. I put the book down and closed my eyes. In a few moments, I was back aboard that train again, watching the metal-cornered black suitcase come toward me. The pain in my head was sharp at first, but it eased away to nothing as I continued to feel myself sliding again into sleep. Sleep, as Jerry noted—*There!*

What's-his-name's name had popped back again!—was becoming my middle name. I'd always enjoyed it, but the concussion had made me a grandmaster. Sleep made up the biggest part of my days.

SIX

"HELLO THERE, BENNY! How are you?" The voice came from a distance. It was familiar, but I couldn't quite place it until I sat up in bed. "You're looking great. You're not pulling a fast one, are you?"

Then a second voice added: "This is a good-sized room you've got here for just the two of you." They were two Toronto cops in plain clothes: Staff-Sergeants Jim Boyd and Jack Sykes of the Toronto Police. Their names weren't available to me when I first saw them, but they returned later as the visit continued. The term "plain clothes" mustn't be taken literally. In my experience plainclothes cops in Ontario usually dressed like hunters just out of the bush. Heavy boots, wool stockings, a growth of beard, jackets with fluorescent red markings, and wool caps. Snowshoes were optional. In a hospital corridor they stood out like moose in tutus or giraffes in a boardroom. The detectives and I had worked a case a year ago. Maybe two.

"Brought you a magazine." Jack Sykes set it down

carefully at the foot of my bed. He handled the copy of *Time* as though his acquaintance with print was recent, which I knew wasn't true. I put it down to nervousness. Both policemen looked at me like I was dressed in a cheap tuxedo and laid out in my coffin. They couldn't look away fast enough.

"At least you're not being broiled alive in here," Boyd commented.

"There's some sort of eclipse going on out there," Sykes noted. Both cops looked at the window. "The sky's still dark from it," he added.

I remembered thinking, not half an hour earlier, about the approaching sunset and noticing the ruddy glow against the hospital windows across the street. I was no longer a fair and accurate observer. Even the simple coming and going of daylight had me confused.

I tried to cross my legs under the coverlet without success. Sykes was admiring the ceiling plaster, Boyd was examining the treasures on the table beside my bed. The attempts at conversation had stopped and we were locked together in heavy silence. Finally, Sykes shook his head at his partner and straightened up. Boyd sighed, then nodded. He had been shifting from one flat foot to the other, eager to be anywhere but here. Sykes ran his big fingers around the rim of the straw hat he was holding close to his body. He looked like a man caught taking a floral tribute away from a funeral because he'd never found the right moment to put it down on the coffin.

It's funny about hospital rooms. Some people never can

relax in them. Even as visitors, they stand woodenly, speak unnaturally, and leave at the first opportunity. Maybe they see the hospital bed as a deathbed. Maybe it's the subdued indirect lighting at the head of the bed, and the equipment for taking blood pressure, supplying oxygen. Any patient unlucky enough to be here is obviously not long for this world. I decided to try to put them at their ease. I cleared my throat, loudly. They both blinked.

"Am I glad to see you guys," I said. Sykes's mouth dropped open. It was like he hadn't expected the body in the coffin to answer back. "I'm going stir-crazy in here."

Boyd and Sykes looked at one another. Both of them glared back at me in the bed.

"I know," I said, "I don't sound like I've got a badly functioning noggin, but I have. Ask my nurse. She'll tell you. I've got a hole in my head you could lose a dollar's worth of change in."

"He walks, he talks, he philosophizes," Sykes said. "What else do you do?" This was more like the cop I knew than the man shifting his feet.

"That's all I can do. But when has talk got any work done? I want to get out of here as fast as I can."

"Hold on, Benny." Sykes said. "We were just talking to the *nurse,* Mrs McKay. You're not getting out of hospital for a long time yet."

"Have you found my car?"

"You don't need a car right now. What you need is rest. Rest and physiotherapy."

"What's the matter with you two? I need to get back on the street."

"Benny, these aren't your local streets. You're in our parish and you haven't got a local media czar making things awkward for us. That was last time; this is now. Best thing you can do is listen to your doctors."

"So, the car *has* turned up!"

"Didn't say one way or the other."

"If it hadn't, you wouldn't have looked at one another the way you just did. And you would have used the fact that it was still missing as an argument to keep me in this bed. Come on, fellows, give me a break. Help me get out of here!"

Again they exchanged glances.

"We'll keep you briefed, Benny. That's the best we can do. There wasn't much to go on, you know. They clobbered you, lifted you into a Dumpster behind Clarendon House, at the corner of Spadina and Wessex, and drove your car behind Barberian's Steak House on Elm Street."

"That's all you got?"

For a moment, the boys looked as guilty as trapped grave robbers. And then the moment passed.

"Benny, we are working on it. Okay? We got a couple of clues we're working up over at forensics. It's still early days."

I didn't mention the fact that now I had a vague idea of how long ago it had happened. "What sort of clues?"

"Get real, Benny! Let us get on with our jobs."

"That's right. We just dropped in to see how you were progressing," his partner chimed in.

"Are you interested in what I can remember about all this?"

Sykes's eyes narrowed. "Sure we are. What were you doing? Who were you messing with? What do you remember?" They looked at me with expectation written on their faces like jam on a six-year-old's.

"Not a blessed thing."

Sykes gave a low wheeze that was intended as a whistle.

"I don't remember who hired me, when I came to Toronto, or why I was hanging around that Dumpster, *if* I was hanging around that Dumpster. Sorry, fellows. I've just come out into the light a little while ago, and I honestly can't remember a damned thing. Yesterday I couldn't tell you my own name. Today is better, but I still have a long way to go."

"We'll leave you our numbers in case it starts coming back to you. Because you're the only living witness to"— here his partner cleared his throat—"to what happened that day."

"What have you got going on the front burners?"

"Benny, we're giving *this* our best shot."

"Yeah, a mugging outranks trespassing on vacant lots and running a red light."

"There's something doing at one of the colleges," Sykes added.

"Which one? There are so many these days, I can't keep up."

"Simcoe College. You know it? Buried behind Massey College?"

"What little I know about higher education in Grantham is enough. Here, I'm really lost."

The boys shook my hand and moved toward the door. When they got there Sykes turned around and casually asked: "Oh, Benny, did you ever know a Flora McAlpine?"

This was a curious parting shot. Must be important. I thought about both the name and the question. It took a few seconds, but no buzz of recognition stirred my consciousness.

"Nothing comes to mind. But then, names aren't my party trick these days. Why?"

"Just wondered whether it sounded familiar. You think about it. Maybe something will stir in there. And you'll let me know?"

"Sure," I said. The question left me with an odd feeling. It was like an echoing ping from the battered back of my head. I wrote the name down before I forgot it. Big or little, important or frivolous: I was capable of forgetting them all. The mention of the name came shortly after talk about one of the university colleges. Was there a connection?

After the boys left, I was alone with my roomie's snoring. I couldn't get peeved at Sykes and Boyd. They couldn't help me to get out of the hospital. Besides, having me where they knew how to find me gave their investigation the only flicker of light they had. And I had enough on my plate just keeping the days of the week straight. I thought of the progress I had made in my reading. In ten or fifteen minutes, I could work my way through a paragraph of six lines. Lucky I wasn't working this case. At my speed I would have it wound up by the time Sykes and Boyd got their pensions.

SEVEN

MOM AND DAD walked through the doorway, Ma in front with a big smile on her face, the kind that hides the pain underneath, and Pa a step or two behind her with his good poker face giving nothing away. She was wearing her Paris Star dress from Montreal, and Dad was dressed more casually in a rust-coloured summer jacket, which he removed as soon as he sat down. Funny how I recognized the dress! It occupied a place of honour in her closet.

"So! At last you've decided to wake up!" Mom gave my foot a squeeze under the covers. "Every time we've been in to see you, you've been off chasing rainbows."

"Hi, there!" Pa said, trying to find the right tone. "You've got a good room here: nice and bright. And you're missing absolutely nothing outside."

"Benny, it's earthquake weather out there. A steam bath. It's spooky. Not only is it hot enough to melt the streets, there was an eclipse of the sun earlier. It'll be blood on the moon next. No wonder people are superstitious about eclipses. There was an eclipse in Rome the day Julius Caesar was murdered. Eclipses are the heart of everything unnatural. They bother my old bones."

"The melting asphalt on the street doesn't make things better."

"You're right, it's frightening out there. But you've at least got a good view of it." Ma looked for a place to put her purse. In the end she held on to it. She kept on talking: "An eclipse of the sun is a terrible thing, Benny."

Pa brought out a cigar, then pocketed it again. "Moon," Pa corrected. "It's a lunar eclipse."

"Well, lunar or solar, it's making this hot weather worse. I saw people crossing themselves."

"What do they know that we don't know? I ask you," Pa said.

"Manny, it doesn't get dark during a lunar eclipse. It has to be dark *before* it happens."

"The moon comes in front of the sun, right? So it's the moon doing the eclipsing. You have to take it logically step by step." Pa took out the cigar again.

"So then a solar eclipse is what? When the sun comes between the earth and the moon? What other nonsense are you selling today?" Ma gave me a look to see if I was on her side.

"There was a program on television about it. You have to be careful of your eyes. You have to use smoked glass."

"Smoked glass?" Ma looked exasperated. "Who's got time to be smoking glass in this weather? Herring I could understand."

Ma moved closer to the bed, while Pa raked his memory about what he had heard about the exact nature of eclipses. Ma studied my face, looking for cracks.

"How is my boy, eh?" Ma asked. "Are you comfortable? I hope you're eating. I know that hospital food is not Lindy's in New York or even the old Diana Sweets in Grantham, but you have to keep your strength up. I only wish they'd let me bring you a bowl of decent soup."

"I think you're allowed to bring in food," I said, trying to be helpful.

"Sure! I'd like to make you some of my beef and barley soup, but how can I make it this far from home? Sam's wife won't let me step inside her tiny, perfect kitchen. I might drop a carrot on her floor. I'm sure she thinks I'm too ethnic for her neighbours."

"Ma, that's just not true."

"Just *you* try to make a cup of instant with her looking on." She exhaled her hostility audibly.

Once Ma had ridden out the storm of guilt she goes through when she's not preparing my meals, things were like old times. Pa told me who among our old neighbours in Grantham had passed on over the spring, and Ma kvetched about hearing the bad news all over again. I think it's what we do instead of crossing ourselves. It works the same way.

"Saul Segal was a healthy man, able to lift those big bolts of factory cotton from his truck to the back of the store without flinching, and then, poof!" Pa said.

"Saul was a good provider," Ma added. "I'll give him

that. But he made too big a thing about all those health foods. Remember, Benny, how he used to tell you not to eat so many chocolate bars?"

I tried remember Saul Segal's face. I recalled a steel jaw and curly brown hair. It was because of him that I gave up chocolate bars and switched to Player's Medium cigarettes. It took me ten years to get rid of *that* habit.

My parents stayed until I began to yawn noticeably. It wasn't that I didn't enjoy their company; it was that their company made me relax and relaxation made me sleepy. I watched the silences grow longer and longer. At last, looking at his watch rather theatrically, Pa said, "Well ..." And I knew that the back of the visit was broken.

Before leaving, my parents passed on the good wishes of our friends in Grantham, and then they were off in an exchange of words about which elevator was closest to the parking lot.

A nurse came into the room without making a sound and took away the accumulated garbage from the waste-bin near my bed. Then, just as silently, she emptied the bin sitting next to my still-sleeping roommate. I call her a nurse, because she looked like a nurse, even though I understood the ranks were actually more subtly sub-divided. One "nurse" I greeted was called Dr Godbehere by a passing woman in uniform. The nurse doing garbage duty was the one who brought me juice and cookies. When she saw me watching her, she said she was glad to see me looking well, called me "Mr Cooperman," and left the room as silently as she had come in. A few minutes later, two nurses from the Islands greeted one another in the corridor with lyrical voices that carried the sun in them.

I wondered if *my* nurse was from down there too. Funny, I hadn't thought about that until just now. When I was helpless in my hard bed, I didn't see colour, but now that I was coming to myself again, some of society's assumptions were returning.

A man in a wheelchair passed my door, using one foot to propel his rig along the corridor. His face was ghostly pale, but he seemed happy to be making his own way.

The next time I got up, after one of my short naps, I went on a tour of the floor. The nursing station in the middle of the corridor divided the floor into unequal halves. One bank of elevators stood here and another at the south end. There were fewer than twenty rooms, most of them double. Across from the nursing station was a dining room with under a dozen tables seating four or six each. A TV set blared above—an inane quiz show, by the look of it. Only one woman in a wheelchair was watching. From time to time she addressed the tube with her sharp comments. A couple of robust-looking men, speaking in French, pushed a comrade dressed in the same familiar hospital outfit: two hospital gowns, one reversed to cover the rear, and a cotton bathrobe. When they caught up to me, they stopped and congratulated me in accented English for being out of bed at last, then continued along the passage.

Having walked from the north end of the floor to the south, I felt like an old political power broker touring the familiar ward and finding that the faces on the street still smiled back at him. While I was exploring, none of the nurses seemed to mind that I wasn't in my room. Access to the elevators was not restricted. I thought that if I had my pants on, I might be able to skip out of the hospital without raising an eyebrow. I filed the idea for later use.

For now, with the slippers on my feet and the two hospital gowns I was wearing, the one letting the draft in through the back and the other allowing errant breezes through the front, it was impossible to contemplate. I might be able to walk up and down the hallway with the assurance of a crocodile, but I recognized that I was not quite ready to brave the out-of-doors. Even in my own clothes, I would need more time.

"So this is where you've got to, is it? Did you see the eclipse?" It was Rhymes With, the nurse from this morning. Or was it yesterday morning?

"I was getting a breath of air," I tried to explain.

"That's good! Some of us went up on the roof to watch it," she said.

"Watch what?"

"The eclipse. That's what everybody's talking about."

"I thought the sun was going down."

"This early? Don't I wish!" She sighed dramatically. "But right now I need some blood."

"*Blood?*"

"Won't take a minute. You'll get used to us claiming bits and pieces of you. I'll come by your room in five minutes. When did you have your blood pressure checked last?"

"When I had the tires rotated. I don't know. If you don't keep track of these things, am I supposed to?"

"Might help. You have to be your own advocate around here, Mr Cooperman. It's the only way to be sure. I tell everybody that, and they laugh. But I'm not joking. See you in five minutes."

I watched her move along the hallway and around a corner. Back in my room, my roommate was sleeping. I decided to clean my teeth. All the while, I was thinking of how I might escape the confines of these walls.

My nurse returned, as she had warned me, with her needle. She was also carrying a hefty notebook, which she passed over to me. "This belonged to a patient who didn't get a chance to really get it started. It's a Memory Book."

"What's a Memory Book?"

"Something to jot down appointments and dates in. Something to give your memory a kick-start. Keep it with you and get rid of those little scraps of paper you write on. Believe me, the Memory Book is better." It looked like most high-school notebooks: black leather cover, three rings, lined paper, unmarked section dividers.

Blankly, I thanked her.

"You'll soon get in the habit of using it. It can even be made to tell you what day of the week it is. Let it become your memory. Let it help you." She gave me a warm smile, which made me feel good. For the first time, I noticed that she had freckles on her cheeks under the light brown pigmentation. I felt a stab of affection for her. I couldn't think of this place without her. Or me without her.

She took blood next. I have to admit that she jabbed a painless needle. Then I tried to read *The Globe and Mail*. It was no good. At some level, I kept hoping that the next thing I tried to read would be easier. It never was. I tried to sound out the words and the meanings of the headlines. "Con ... Coined ... Council ... Ignores ... Idiot ... Injects ... Ann ... Andrew ... Angry ..." I took a breath and tried again. Eventually, I made out: "COUNCIL EJECTS ANGRY COUNSELLOR." I had no difficulty with the sense of the words once I had decoded them. Language wasn't my problem; it was breaking the alphabet code that dogged my progress.

I could feel a nap coming on. But I made time to put my name and address on the Memory Book I'd been given. I used the calendar provided to note what day of the week and month this was. The information dissolved almost at once, but it did give me a buzz while I was able to hold on to it. After another five-minute struggle with the front page, I gave up and added my own snores to those of my roommate.

EIGHT

A PARADE OF DAYS PASSED, with muffled drums, not at all dissimilar to the days I've just described. The only difference was that the days, however long they seemed at the time, appeared to blend in to one another and get lost. The days dragged themselves through weeks that flew. Today might be clear and in focus, but yesterday is the distant past. Almost an abstraction. I could no longer remember whether I had had visits from my doctor, from my parents, or from my police friends yesterday morning. Or was it the Saturday before?

"Will you be eating your dinner in your room tonight as usual, Mr Cooperman, or would you like to join the others in the dining room?" It was the silent nurse who always called me by name.

"I think I'll try the dining room. How will I know when they're serving?"

"You'll see the others pass your doorway, Mr Cooperman. If you miss them, we'll come and collect you." Something to look forward to.

I tried to keep track of the days of the week, as posted in large letters and figures in the dining room, but the days seemed to scatter like those montage sequences in old movies where the leaves blow off the calendar to show the passage of time. It had been three weeks since I "woke up." Or maybe it was six. Or longer. I had no strong belief in any of my opinions. People kept telling me that it was longer. I wasn't counting the time I couldn't remember. I couldn't even imagine it. What was it that Englishman wrote in his book about intrigue in a stately home before the First World War? "The past is a foreign country. They do things differently there." Something like that. I was looking at time through the wrong end of a telescope.

I soon became regular in my attendance at meals. The dining room was a large, well-lighted room across the hall from the nursing station. Some of us arrived at the tables long before the food reached the fifth floor in the elevator. It came out the sliding doors with a metallic clatter and puffs of steam. The servers quickly emptied the noisy carts into the dining room. It was a sound of joy to the newcomers, whose first out-of-room meal this was, and an occasion for complete indifference to old-timers, who had learned to limit their expectations.

Among the most enthusiastic of the old-timers were the three Belgians, who had struck up quite a friendship since their strokes had flung them together. One was a retired engineer, who now had trouble remembering numbers; another was a former mover-and-shaker in the sublime upper reaches of financial policy for the World Bank; and the third was the curator, now retired, of a major art gallery. He did not say which one, but from his conversation, I could tell that he had seen them all. These three entertained one another and those nearby, since they always spoke English, with stories about the best meals they had eaten in the best restaurants around the globe. They argued about whether this or that great table had maintained its standards in the last few years, or whether everything had gone downhill after Madam or Maître Charles had died.

There were women on this floor too, of course, only I didn't get to know many of them. There was the real estate broker who was something of a celebrity since she had returned to this floor with her second stroke. And there was the older woman who argued with the people on the TV screen.

My scant acquaintance with the great tables of Europe tended to limit my contributions to the conversation. Not only did I not know much about the favourite eateries in Paris, London, Brussels, and Rome, I didn't know much about the fancy dishes they were talking about. I had heard of foie gras and frogs' legs, but I couldn't really keep up with their repertoire. And when they turned to the great wines of the world and were joined by a former United Nations representative from Prague, I decided that listening and keeping quiet was the better part of valour.

"Not far from Chopin's little retreat at Nohant, near La Châtre in Berri, there's a village called Vic. Best lunch I ever had in Europe. For simplicity, for originality ..."

"Come now!"

"It's true! I insist! Such care! Such attention to detail! Ah, I grow weak just thinking about it."

"My dear friend, you haven't lived until you have eaten at Chez Georges not a block from the unjustly celebrated Coq d'Or in Nîmes."

"Unjustly celebrated? Ah, but you didn't know it when the old man was still alive. Big as a mountain, he was, and he kept that kitchen in order, I'll tell you. Never have I eaten such chicken. And his salads! Cyrano's friend, Ragueneau, the pastry chef in the play, could have written sonnets praising his sauces alone." And so on. The conversation was as animated as though we were sitting in a five-star restaurant, surrounded by the greatest living chefs. Sitting among this group of world travellers were patients who commented with looks and shrugs across the table. One of these, I think, was a former judge, another was a trial lawyer, famous in stories my father told. Meanwhile, just so you don't get the idea that this was some sort of gourmets' retreat, the rest of the patients stared into their bowls without uttering a word, or if they did, it was about something they were watching on the television screen which, as far as I could see, had no off switch.

"So *here* you are, you sly old fox!" It was the nurse who spelled off the one whose name I couldn't remember. I couldn't remember her name either. "You didn't tell us you were married."

"I didn't tell you I was married because I'm not. Do you mean my friend, Anna? Anna's as close as I get to a wife." A cloud ran across the nurse's eyes, as if the joke she had been about to make had melted in her mouth. My companions leaned in closer.

"Are you saying you *aren't* married?" asked the nurse.

"Not now and never have been, so help me."

"Well, that's odd."

"What's so odd? It's not bothered me much. Has it become compulsory?"

"I was talking to Erna Pyke. You know, she runs the desk when Libby's off. Anyway, she told me that a week or so ago you had a visit from your wife. She said she lived in Grantham and everything."

"And it wasn't Anna Abraham? My friend, Anna Abraham?"

"Not according to Libby. And she knows Dr Abraham."

"I've never heard of a Dr Abraham." This was the contribution of one of the gourmets. I explained that Anna was an academic friend of mine. She had been more than a friend for a long time, but we'd retreated from that advanced position some time ago. He didn't have to know about that. He shrugged his indifference.

"Maybe I shouldn't have brought this up at the table, Mr Cooperman. I'm sorry."

"See if you can find out what my wife is supposed to have looked like. Maybe she was just trying to get in?"

"I'm sorry. I didn't mean to embarrass you."

"I'm not embarrassed. I'm intrigued but not embarrassed. I'd like to know more. Like when this happened and what did she look like."

"I'll see what I can do. And ... I'm *really* sorry."

"What was that all about? Are you married or not?" asked the retired engineer to my right.

"If it's any of our business," added the diplomat.

"Right," said the banker. "We don't mean to pry."

"It's just as much of a mystery to me as it is to you." I didn't tell them what I was thinking. Was it someone trying to finish the job started in the Dumpster, or was a new character in this tangled tale making a dramatic entrance? I wanted to find out. But I didn't know where to begin.

NINE

I MISSED ANNA ABRAHAM. All the talk about my mysterious "wife" made me wish Anna would come to see me. I understood from the nurses that Anna had sometimes come up to the fifth floor, but that I had been off in cloud-cuckoo-land. One of the young cleaners, who, I gathered, had encountered Anna while mopping my room, shook his head at me, saying, "I hope I'm never *that* tired."

On the question of visitors I was insatiable. Professional visitors as well as personal ones—I couldn't get enough of them. When company was in short supply, I became greedy for more. I became a company junkie; I wanted a line of visitors at the door. But it seemed to me that my neighbour, Jerry, saw more visitors than I did.

Then it hit me that I might be under police protection. What if the Dumpster Gang came back to finish the job. Could anybody walk in to see me? Would the nurses opposite the elevator give anybody my room number? My "wife" didn't seem to have had much trouble.

One day, I followed one of the nurses into the elevator and pushed the button for the main floor. Not a word was said. No one lifted a hand to bar my way. I felt proud of myself as I stood in my dressing gown facing the unrestricted front door.

"Are you busy?" It was Anna Abraham, my sometime girlfriend, whom I hadn't seen since I don't remember when.

"Anna! God, I'm glad to see you! How did you find me?" Anna took a breath, as though I'd just asked an impossible question. "Oh, I know all about your secret life. I watch at keyholes, tap phones, read tea leaves, interpret bumps and warts. For weeks I've been studying your face in repose."

"I know that," I said. "How did you *first* hear?"

"There was a piece in the paper. The *Beacon*. Besides, I have my spies. You're not the only one who can dig up the facts. Remember, I'm a trained researcher as well as a professor. How are you feeling?"

"I thought I'd never see you again."

"I'm not that easy to dump, Benny. I stick like burrs to your pant leg."

"I missed you." It was true. It seemed like a thousand years since I'd gazed at the wonderful structure of her cheekbones. And yet I retained the shadow of a memory of an earlier visit. Had she been here, or was it only in my dreams?

"You told me so last week when I was here."

"You were here to see me? My head's a bit thick, Anna. Humour me." Sometime the bread you cast upon the waters washes back with the first wave; she gave me a big kiss.

"I've been in and out a few times. You just don't remember, that's all. It's not your fault. Besides, I some-times catch you having a nap. I like watching you sleep. It's very restful. Did I say that before? Sorry. I've been missing your peculiar bachelor ways: rolled socks in the bread box, trousers under the mattress." Her voice was brittle, like glass.

"If you give me a minute, I'll put my pants on and we can go for a walk," I said. She grinned as I rolled free of my hospital corners. While I was busy finding my trousers and getting into them, a thought crossed my mind: was Anna holding something back? The clue was in her bright banter. Something more than bedside manner. It reminded me of my conversations with my brother Sam and Staff-Sergeant Sykes. Something was off balance and it wasn't just me.

In ten minutes, we were sitting in the café in the hospital. I had my Memory Book beside me; I felt secure. Anna was at the counter buying coffee and talking to a tall stranger with a summer hat in his hands. I held our table against all comers. And there were a few. I was beginning to wonder at my growing passivity; why wasn't I collecting the drinks and paying the shot?

Anna put a tray on the table. "Fellow up there wanted to know if I wished to make ten thousand dollars," she said.

"Sounds like a good scam. Did you take him up on it?"

"No. I told him I was more interested in spiritual values. I got him involved in a long religious discussion.

That stopped him." She unloaded the coffee and two oatmeal cookies. After getting rid of the tray, she sat down across from me and leaned forward. "Now," she said. "Tell me what's new."

As briefly as I could, I brought her up to date on the treatment I was having to get over the trauma. I told her about my newly imposed regimen. I was now being shunted around the hospital to classes in three kinds of therapy. In physical therapy I had to walk on an irregular ramp to test my balance, climb up and down a flight of stairs, and spend twenty minutes riding a stationary bicycle. Occupational therapy tested me with games to see how deep my brain damage went.

"The third class is in reading," I explained. "Here the teacher, a Miss ... Sorry, her name escapes me. Anyway, she tries to re-educate my poor bruised brain to recognize the letters of the alphabet again and the words they could be organized to form. I'm slow at this; the letters keep changing shape on me, *r*'s becoming *p*'s without warning and *j*'s turning into *h*'s." I could find no sense in this. If the *d*'s suddenly became *b*'s, or the *p*'s, *q*'s, I could see the dyslexic logic of my degeneration. Maybe I was foolish to look for method in my confusion. My disorganized head treated all letters equally; my affliction was at least democratic.

I also told Anna how anxious I was to get back on the street again. I even included what I could remember of the more upbeat of the comments that had been made by doctors and nurses in passing. When I had finished, she sat back hard in her chair.

"Wow! Poor bunny, you really have been raked over the broken glass, haven't you? Everything but wild dogs chasing you over frozen ice floes."

"Hell, no! I'm just a member of the walking wounded. My floor is full of people who can't walk or talk or put a spoon in their mouth. I'm one of the lucky ones. I'm so fit they may be getting rid of me before too long."

"But your reading? Your memory?"

"Neither will be cured by bedrest here on the fifth floor. There are people here who can't even pull the bell cord to call a nurse if they need one."

"Whoever attacked you can claim 'by way of mitigation' that he could have hit you harder."

"We have to catch him first. Do you know the university residence at the corner of Wessex and Spadina?"

"The building with the crazy O dangling over traffic? Sure."

"Could you nose around the Dumpster and see if the perpetrator left his name and address anywhere?"

"Benny! Two things: you're forgetting how long ago this attack on you occurred, and I'm a lecturer in English literature, not Susanna of the Mounties. I wouldn't even know what to look for."

"You're right. I keep forgetting you're not Batgirl. Besides, aren't there students waiting for you to show up at Secord?"

"No, not during the summer, Benny. Instead, I'm teaching summer school here on Tuesdays and Thursdays. Coming here to visit you doesn't take me out of my way at all. In fact, it helps me pass the time. It keeps me out of libraries and such low places. Let me think about your idea overnight."

"Forget it, Anna. It was a dumb idea. Even *I* have them sometimes."

"Do you really think I might find something?"

"It's just part of the drill. It's unlikely there's anything to find, but you can't check it off the list of things to do if you haven't looked."

"I'll see what I can do."

"Thanks, Anna. It's just that I'm going stir-crazy in here. I need to be up and doing already. The longer I stay in bed, the weaker I get."

Anna took my hand across the table. "Damn your wheedling ways, Benny. I should be armed against them at this late date in our relationship. I'll go around there and have a closer look. I'll see what I can find. And if I run into what Flora McAlpine ran into, I'll take my lumps."

"Who's Flora McAlpine? The cops asked me about her."

"Didn't they *tell* you?"

"Tell me *what*? The name rings a very distant bell."

"Flora McAlpine was a professor at the university. She was lying in the Dumpster with you. They found the two of you together. The only difference was that you were still alive and Professor McAlpine was dead."

TEN

ANNA AND I WALKED across the hospital lobby. It was busy, crowded with people frustrated in one way or another. They couldn't find where a patient was located, or they couldn't find a proper gift for some newborn. Vaguely I admired the volunteers who tried to treat each request, however confused, with cool clarity and simplicity.

We walked outside and found a wooden bench facing a children's playground. The toys inside the enclosure—tricycles, wagons, and kiddy-cars—were mostly broken, mangled by use or neglect.

"Tell me about it," I said at last.

"There's not much to tell. Didn't your police friends ...?"

"Not a word. Just her name as they went out the door. They must have been testing me. I don't know."

"Flora McAlpine was a teacher at one of the colleges. Properly, she was *Doctor* Flora McAlpine. She was forty-five, unmarried, and by all accounts a good teacher. She lived in Clarendon House. She also had a head injury, same as you, but hers was fatal. I don't know any more than that, Benny. I'm sorry."

By the time Anna delivered me back to my room, I was completely exhausted. I was less than my usual affable self when I pecked her on the cheek and waved her away. The ping of the elevator bell sounded with finality as she vanished. My shirt was wet through across the shoulders and down my back.

I must have broken some speed record when I pulled the bedcovers around me and surrendered myself to forty winks that lasted through the whole of the late afternoon. I slept through both speech and occupational therapy, waking only when the occupational therapist came to see if I was still breathing.

"I've been out for a walk," I explained. "My first, as far as I remember. Sorry I missed those classes. Can I make them up in some way?" The young woman, whose name I still managed to forget, instructed me in hospital policy, and I returned to sleep for another half hour. It seemed to me that most of my day was pieced together from naps and rests and sleeps and lie-downs of varying seriousness. I guess there was healing going on somewhere in my head and I needed more sleep than normal. When I finally woke up, it was close to dinnertime. The whole day, like so many that had gone before it, had fled like retreating guerrillas before a massed attack of infantry with armoured support.

Dinnertime found me with the gourmets at the table farthest from the television set. The Czech who'd been a

United Nations representative was there too, and he turned out to have an interest in crime fiction. I'd read a bit myself, and so I encouraged him in his attempts to move the conversation away from the best place in the Dordogne to find a truly outstanding cassoulet. My new friend shut the others up saying that nobody in the Dordogne has any business looking for a cassoulet in the first place. He'd be better off looking for a superior hot dog. We all laughed, but one of the gourmet crowd was mildly injured by the remark.

I became anxious after dinner. When I had eliminated all the other possible sources, I was troubled by the knowledge that Anna might be poking around that university residence on her own. I was anxious both for her personal safety and for the scraps of information she might have come across. Anna had helped me out in the past, but usually I was with her or the situation was less sinister.

Under the surface of my concern for Anna's fair hide was a large ration of guilt about the way our close relationship had stalled. There had been no way to turn my job into a nine-to-five operation, and I had missed more dates and appointments. To stay alive a relationship has to grow and expand, or it dies of neglect. One night, looking in a drawer for a stamp, I found a clutch of theatre tickets that she had bought for the two of us. In each case I failed to show up. And through it all, she pretended to shrug off my habitual delinquency. Anna was a remarkable woman.

I wondered whether I could slip away from the hospital long enough to make sure she was safe. By day, she would be fully visible to all; by night, her flashlight might attract the U of T campus police. Or she might surprise the guy who hit me.

I stopped myself. This was my bum head talking. Anna was in no danger; my encounter with the Dumpster was weeks—no, months—ago. Why couldn't I hold on to that fact? Why did my ideas now have big holes in them?

None of this helped to relax me. Thank God, my Czech friend from the dinner table came by and asked me whether I would like to play chess. As luck would have it, I did play. The odd thing was that he seemed to know that already. I wondered whether my brain injury would give me an advantage over my partner, who had suffered a crippling stroke. The next few hours passed by quickly as I demonstrated to my friend just how badly I played the game. And as for my earlier worries about Anna, they vanished for a time as the fate of my beleaguered queen had to be dealt with.

After my new friend left, the worries returned. The outing with Anna got me thinking about life outside. Did the hospital have a course on reintegrating former patients into their neglected lives? Or was the Memory Book all I could hope for? How would I learn to pay my bills with my trick memory? How could I remember the names of my clients? I pictured one sitting across from me, telling me her problems, while my problem was trying to remember the name she gave me. I *could* install a blackboard on the wall facing me. Here I could enter the names of my clients. The client wouldn't see it, and it would help bolster my assurance. The idea made me feel better, and I began to invent other ways to make life away from University Avenue supportable.

My new life was going to depend on such strategies: the Memory Book, pocket notebooks, and diaries. I was at last going to have to get organized, as my teacher Miss MacDoughal kept warning me back in grade four. It was going to be a peculiar life, I had to admit: part of my old memory worked—I could still remember about the Battle of Hastings and when Julius Caesar crossed his Rubicon—but I could no longer remember the names of my many first cousins. While I was trying to list all sixteen of them, I had the haunting feeling that I had done this before. I didn't so much mind the duplication of the work as I did the feeling that I was looking over my own shoulder to see what was going on. I could remember Anna and her father, but I had lost his first name. And in order to remember his last name, I had to go back to Anna's, which, of course, was the same. I kept surprising myself with my own ingenuity; for instance, I was trying to recall the name Grant for some reason. I spent ten minutes going through the alphabet searching for the name. I succeeded only when I remembered that I'd once worked for a Saul Granofsky, whose daughters had changed their name to Grant. My memory was full of such filigrees of twisted silken strands. My new memory required me to build a latticework of aids to criss-cross my experience and expectation.

ELEVEN

THERE WERE DAYS and days of tests. Some were simply physical, like the blood pressure monitor I wore around my arm for twenty-four hours. Every so often it would begin to squeeze my arm like a persistent python, then release me after a minute: a silent companion who followed me everywhere. I was able to take more pride in the tests of my mental functions. They were more involving. I was childishly delighted in my correct answers, but the seeds of depression were planted with every incorrect response.

"That was excellent, Mr Cooperman. You got them all."

"I wish I could read faster."

"That'll come. With practice and time." The therapist that day was a woman in her late twenties. She had a pleasant manner; I didn't feel as though I were being made to jump through hoops. She never spoke about me to another therapist while I was standing there listening. When the therapist left, I'd continue the conversation with my nurse.

"Should I be doing something about my reading?"

"You're going to speech therapy twice a week."

"I know, but isn't there something more I could be doing?"

"Have you tried reading a book?"

"It takes me all day to get through *The Globe and Mail*. A book could hang me up until the Second Coming."

"Get along with you! You're doing very well here. But I thought you were Jewish, Mr Cooperman."

"I was. I mean, I *am;* but when it comes to measuring the time it will take me to recover my old reading speed, the phrase seemed appropriate. What could be longer than an unbeliever's idea of the Second Coming?"

"You've got a point."

"Do you think I'll ever be able to read again?"

"I've seen all sorts of progress on this floor, Mr Cooperman."

"Call me Benny."

"And you've forgotten my name again."

"I forget it *all* the time. I know it rhymes with something, but I can't hold on to it. It's not just you; I can't remember anybody's name. I was never great at names, but this is ridiculous!"

"My name is Carol McKay and it rhymes with 'day.'" She repeated the name and the mantra that went with it. For me at least it was a mnemonic trick with a flat tire. I repeated it with her. I planted it in my heart of hearts and there, a moment after she left the room, it vanished. I felt stupid, as though I'd just listened to an hour-long lecture and come away without a thought in my head and no words to explain what it had been all about. It wasn't that I forgot who she was or that I forgot what she said to me. It was just the name itself.

There was a ringing in my ears. I tried to shake it away, but it persisted.

"Hello?" Jerry, my roommate, waited for a moment while the caller identified himself. I could follow it all. I just hadn't noticed before that I had a phone next to me. Then I remembered my wrangle with the unhelpful telephone operator.

Jerry handed me the receiver, then wheeled himself back to his side of the room.

"Hello? Benny?" It was Anna. "Are you okay? Benny?"

"I've got a phone beside my bed, Anna!"

"I know. I've seen it. Are you okay?"

"Yes, I'm fine. What have you got for me?" I had not forgotten my earlier worries about Anna's safety. I should have asked whether she was still in good health. It would have shown me to be a good and caring friend and sometime lover. But I was more interested in what she had to tell me just then. The bang on the head had rendered me no more considerate than I used to be. I still cut to the chase.

It also hit me that today must be either Tuesday or Thursday, Anna's teaching days in Toronto. Some small things were beginning to stick in my mind again. It was a good feeling.

"Benny, are you still there?"

I cleared my throat. "Sorry, Anna. I was wool-gathering. Is this long distance?"

"No, I'm still in town. Why?"

"No special reason." I heard a sigh descend on me down the telephone line. "I went through the alley where the Dumpster is located. I nosed around, as you like to say ..."

"And?"

"And I felt stupid. I'll be honest, Benny. Too much time has gone by, and the cops have been all over that thing a dozen times. I didn't expect to find anything and I didn't."

"Now that I think of it, I'm not surprised." What really surprised me was the fact that I sent her on such a fool's errand in the first place. The crime scene was cold by the time I came to the rehab. I could feel my energy for this conversation leaching out of me. I tried to hold on. After all, Anna had tried. I owed her for that at least.

"Benny?"

"You shouldn't have gone there alone, Anna."

"You think the guy who conked you and poor Flora is staked out to conk just anybody?"

"No, I just don't want you to get hurt. I couldn't live with myself if something happened to you in a dark alley while I was cooped up in here. It's bad enough being flat on my back; putting you in the way of danger makes me ..."

"Yes?"

"... want to get out of here faster and get back to work." Anna sighed again. Right away, I was sorry I had said that. I cleared my throat and looked out the windows.

"It's not a dark alley. You're thinking of B movies, Benny. There's busy traffic on two sides. Well, almost."

"Just don't take chances. I'm a worrywart where you're concerned."

"Benny, what are you trying to say?"

"There's no coverage for you in my business insurance plan. So don't take any more chances."

"Any other orders?"

"You are going to be here Tuesdays and Thursdays, right?" I was showing off. But if she had asked me whether this was Tuesday, Thursday, or Saturday, I wouldn't have been able to help her. Even without a mind with holes in it, the normal hospital routine tended to make one day seem much like the last. I went on. "Could you get my office key from Frank Bushmill—he's in the office next door to mine—and see what you can discover about my reasons for being in Toronto in the first place? I don't think that you'll get hit over the head on St Andrew Street in Grantham. My desk isn't as tidy as a pin, but I'm sure that you'll be able to sort out my system after a minute or so. Look for the yellow legal-sized pads. Call me from the office phone. Tell Frank that I'm okay, okay? I hate to lumber you with all this, Anna, but I think getting back to work will help me get clear of this place faster."

There were a lot of things to think about. For a minute, I thought, What am I getting so excited for? I don't even have a client! Then I remembered that *I* was the client. And that brought me back to remembering that I was both an idiot and a fool. With that self-revelation stinging my eyes, I said goodbye.

TWELVE

WHILE I WAS WAITING for Anna and for the solution to the secret of the time I had spent in Toronto before my memory took unpaid leave, I tried to make a list of a few of those things that were on my mind. In my Memory Book, I wrote down: *What brought me to Toronto?*

I tried to remember my working habits; would they yield anything useful? During past investigations, I made notes in pencil on lined yellow pads. I'd been doing it that way for years. The word "years," or something about the word, seemed to make a pass at my memory. But it was only a pass. It didn't hold on or turn into something more substantial. Back to the libretto.

I must have made notes on a pad of paper on my desk this time, too. I would ask Anna to look into that when she went back home to Grantham. Or had I already asked her? Did I take these notes with me on my trip to Toronto? It was only rarely that I made a copy of my notes. Maybe the notes were in my car. I had to have it collected from the parking lot behind that restaurant sooner or later anyway. Anna could do that. *No, damn it!* That was asking too much of her! But it *is* less dangerous than having her climb into Dumpsters on her own. I didn't want that girl ending up in some landfill on my account.

What was the connection, if any, with the steak house? A heavy, on the run, might pick the parking lot of a busy restaurant as a place to abandon a car. But if he did so, he'd probably pick one where he had never shown his face before. Waiters have good memories for faces, and a person who parked but didn't pick up the car might have stuck in the memory of a waiter or dishwasher having a smoke out back. Again, I cursed my immobile state. I tried to think of another line to follow up, but couldn't imagine one.

Sleepiness was stealing along my bones. After a brief struggle, I gave up, kicked off my slippers, and closed my eyes.

When I opened my eyes again, Jerry What's-his-name's son was borrowing a chair from near my bed. Jerry was entertaining a large group of people, some of whom I could see through the gaps in the curtains. Jerry's raspy voice was quizzing his son about whether or not a ramp could be built from the driveway to the side door of his house. Dagmar told him not to worry about it, that Joel was in touch both with the builder and with Jerry's doctor. But Jerry was a good detail man, so he continued asking his son about the nuts and bolts. The muffled drone of this conversation, brightened from time to time with sallies of Dagmar's accented soprano, almost put me back

to sleep again. I hoisted myself out of bed, covered my
loins with a terry cloth kimono that I couldn't recall ever
having seen before, even though it was comfortable and
old, and walked toward the dining room. A chess game was
being played: the Czech diplomat against one of the gourmets from Belgium. I stood behind the diplomat and
watched.

"Ha!" said the gourmet at the move of a king-side
pawn. "Remember you did that ten minutes from now!"

"I hope we both remember, my friend," said the diplomat with a suppressed smile. The smile suggested to me
that I might be able to take him in a poker game. But
poker was my father's game. They didn't call him the
Hammer for nothing. I kept watching, even as some of the
ambulatory crowd tired and moved to other activities or
relaxations. I kept on watching. It didn't look as if it was
going to take very long:

WHITE	BLACK
Q-Q3	BxN
PxB	Q-N4ch
K-B1	N-B5!
B-B1	Q-R4
PxP	RxP!!
BxN	RxR!
Q-Q1	RxB!

Here the moment came for my gourmet friend to eat
his words. White was all over Black, as even I could see.

Both players continued to examine the board, as though reserve forces were available underneath the table. Even I could see that if the play had gone QxR/B1, R-KB6! Either way Black wins.

"I've been looking for you!" It was my special nurse. No name, no rhyme, but I did remember that hers was the first face I had seen as I came out of the black hole of my wanderings between the world of the 4:15 train and the other side. I held out my hand for the plastic cup with the pill in it. I downed the pill with one swallow. It amused me to realize that I was, in a small way, proud of my accomplishment. In hospital, I'd become simple and childish; I enjoyed praise and the successful execution of small tasks.

The cheerful laughter of two other nurses or orderlies made the smile grow. I was strangely happy about the chess game, about the nurse's care of me, and about the peal of laughter from the West Indies. They all supported me, I thought, and this wasn't such a bad place to be after all.

To celebrate this new feeling of optimism, I walked down the corridor, passed the elevators at the nursing station, and went to the block of elevators at the sunny south end of the building. The elevator door opened and I was in Grantham again. I knew the man standing inside.

"Benny?" he said.

"Bud!" It was Bud Phelan from home.

As I stepped into the elevator, we both said, "What are *you* doing here?" at the same time.

Bud scratched his grey hair and explained that he was in town with his barbershop quartet to perform upstairs for the patients with aphasia and had got separated from the other three. He told me he was the tenor. It was good to see that I could still recognize a familiar face, even when it popped up out of its usual context. We got out in the lobby. Here Bud found his companions. Meanwhile I strained my mind to remember that seeing Bud didn't mean I was back in Grantham. And why, I wondered, did I recognize him out of the blue, when I couldn't remember the name of my own nurse? This memory scar had irregular edges.

When I got to the big front door, I looked at the poor wretches out in the street, smiling to myself. While they were still caught up in the rat race, I was, for the foreseeable future, blanketed from all the crazy things going on out there. It was a good, warm feeling. My surroundings and those who peopled it were benign, friendly, and safe.

Back in the elevator, I couldn't remember my floor. *All* of the numbers on the selection panel looked good to me. I picked 3 and tried that. The view through the door as it opened was dim, without sunlight; I remembered that on my floor there was a bright sunlit pattern on the wall facing the elevator. I tried again: 12. The sunlight was better on 12, but the nursing station was wrong, unfamiliar. Through the window at the end of the hall, I saw a glimpse of roof below me. It belonged to an added wing attached to the building, but not rising as high as the one I was in. This roof went only so far. I figured that my floor,

whichever it was, must be the floor at the level immediately above the roof. I could remember roof-y things
through the window: the bumps made by vents and air-
conditioning blower units. I took a stab at the fifth floor,
holding my breath as the car descended. By now I had
company: two nurses and one stretcher with an accompa-
nying supporting stand for plastic sacks of saline solution
running into the unfortunate occupant of the trolley.

Fifth floor! I got it right! I stepped out of the car with
what I hoped looked like authority. I sank into the bed
and soon lost myself in a long nap.

My dreams, since the head injury, tended to be in
black and white. I couldn't remember much about them
afterwards. Often they included bits of the nightmare of
the train tipping over and the suitcase hitting me in the
head. While I was still in bed with my eyes closed, I tried
to remember whether there were any new elements. I
thought that there was something different, but I couldn't
place it. As I rolled over, I remembered the advice a
therapist had given me: let the missing thought slide out
of the centre of attention. The way to winkle out a shy
memory was to give it its head, pay no attention until it
ran into focus.

"These flowers came for you, Mr Cooperman." It was
a nurse with an armful of roses and other flowers. She
was the quiet nurse, the one who never tried to engage me
in conversation. "I'll put them here by the window where
you can see them in the light. Look at those roses! I love
roses, roses of all colours, although I'm partial to pink.

Some people love yellow roses. My daughter, for instance. She dotes on yellow roses. Is that supposed to mean something?" I remembered seeing a book called *The Language of Flowers*. I remembered not opening it, so I couldn't help the nurse as she settled the bouquets in the light from the window. Funny nurse, I thought. I used to think of her as the silent one. But she isn't. She chatters pleasantly.

"I can't find a card, Mr Cooperman. They must be from your secret admirer."

My curiosity must have been dozing. I accepted the flowers as my due. Was I getting very grand in my hospital gown? Probably it was part of the general passivity that the hospital induces in its inmates, a phase of my recuperation.

The nurse stood back, admiring her work, arms akimbo. "Would you like a cookie, Mr Cooperman?" She had been carrying cookies as well as flowers. That seemed funny, somehow. Accepting two cookies from her, I thought of her having to learn all of our names. Dozens of names! Part of the job, I guessed. It was people management. Make them feel like you care.

Where had the cynicism come from? A minute earlier, I'd been thinking of her carrying flowers and cookies, a modern Florence Nightingale. A few minutes ago, everything was rosy. There were no shadows on my roses. Given time and patience, everything would come up roses. Roses, roses all the way! Roses? Rose? I looked at the flowers again. The name seemed to catch in my head. Not just the flower, but the *name* Rose.

It *was* a name, of course, but where had it come from? I tried to comb through my shattered memory for any forgotten Roses. There was a much-loved aunt, but she had died many years ago. Why would her name come to mind just now? I stared at the ceiling with its tracks carrying divider curtains across the room and around the beds. Did this have something to do with my dream?

I repeated the name over and over again in my head. There were no Rosies or Roses in my life as far as I could remember. There were no Roses among the nursing staff. I couldn't remember any of their names, but at the same time I was sure that none of them were Rose or Rosie. I tried to find a face that would go with the name. It wasn't a new or trendy name. It was a nice Victorian name, belonging to the past, suitable for elderly aunts and cousins. At the same time I was thinking this, the face of a young woman crept into my mind. The face was indistinct, vague, incorporeal, but young. Somewhere in her twenties, or maybe in her late teens. It wasn't much and it didn't seem to come out of the train nightmare. She wasn't one of the tumbling shapes in that railway car.

Then it hit me. I was an idiot. This was the Rose of Sharon Rehabilitation Hospital. My life was saved, I guess, right here. No wonder the name Rose had a special meaning for me. I was going to be forever grateful to the Rose of Sharon. No wonder the name occupied such a large place in my shattered memory.

Back to square one.

It wasn't easy to let go of the only clue I had to how I came to be found in Toronto. What was I doing here, why did I come, in whose interest was I clobbered, and how did I lose my mind and car? I tried to get the name out of my head. I tried thinking about who the *Rose of Sharon* was. Why didn't I know the Bible better than I did? Was it New Testament or Old? Was she some pious farm-girl who had visions? Was she a worker of rural miracles or the scourge of unruly kings? There seemed to be a predictable pattern in saints. In early saints, anyway. Useful saints came along later in history: nursing sisters and teachers.

When I woke from my nap—yes, another nap; I seemed to thrive on them—I found the name Rose just as fixed in my mind as it had been earlier. I went over the logic for discarding it, but in the end I came to recognize that the name had a legitimate claim on me. I resolved to quiz Mom and Dad about the name when they returned. There was someone else, too. Someone who knew Grantham's back-stairs history as few others did. However, after trying for five minutes, going through the alphabet a dozen times, I still couldn't remember her name. It was a woman. She had figured in one of my old cases. I'd ask her when her name came to the surface in my battered *pia mater*. She might be of help. If Mom didn't know a Rose, maybe my friend, the Grantham gossip, would. It wasn't much, but it was a start.

"Benny! At *last* you've got your *eyes* open!" It was Mom and Dad. "Every time I look in to see you, you're sleeping. Yesterday I sat here for twenty, twenty-five minutes. Not a blink out of you."

"I'm sorry that I've slept through your visits. It's not very polite."

"Don't fret the easy stuff, Benny. You can't be punished for what happens when you are asleep," Ma protested. "Besides, I haven't seen you sleeping for years. It takes me back to when you were little."

"She sat there looking at you as if you were going to melt, Benny. Tell her you're not going to melt."

"Not that I know of. The air conditioning in here helps." I could see the worry on their faces, but I didn't know how to get them to relax. We haven't had a lot of illnesses in our family, so I didn't have much to build on.

"You'd think it was a plot," Ma said. "As soon as we walk in the door, you fall into a deep sleep. The nurse said, 'Pull his big toe. Squeeze the end of his nose.' But I couldn't do that. Although I used to drag you out of bed when you slept in as a boy."

"Next time, pull my toe. I'm getting plenty of sleep." I had a thought that I hoped would change the subject. "Ma, do I know anyone named Rose or Rosie?"

"There was your poor Aunt Rosie, *olev hasholem*."

"*Besides* Aunt Rosie. Someone above ground, from home. Maybe a school friend or an old girlfriend?"

"Well, I don't know. I used to encourage you and Sam to bring your friends home. Rosie or Rose? I can't think of anything right now. That was all so long ago."

My father was shaking his head too. I let out the breath of hope I had been holding. I'd think of something else.

"You know, you're lucky to have your brother and so many specialists on call, not to mention a ward full of interesting patients. I've been talking to some of them. I played a few hands of gin rummy with a few of them. They all paid up like the gentlemen they are."

"Pa, you took their *money*?"

"That's the game. They'd have taken mine if I'd played as badly as they did. What's a couple of dollars?"

"When you've finished fleecing the patients here on the fifth floor, you can run up to the sixth. You should be able to really clean up there."

"What's on six?"

"Incurables."

Pa blinked and we all sat through a lengthy silence.

Finally, I said, "Ma, did I talk to you before I came to Toronto? Did I tell you anything about why I was coming here?"

"You keep asking me that, Benny. No, you didn't say anything this time any more than you ever do. You hardly ever talk about your work, Benny. I just hope that you're finished with whatever trouble you've got into. Thank God they didn't kill you! You brought your laundry, wouldn't stay for a sandwich, and that was the last I saw of you. You were in a hurry about something."

"But not enough to forget to drop off my dirty underwear. Did I ever mention a girl named Rose or Rosie?"

"Dear, you just asked us that. No, Benny, we don't know of a Rose or Rosie in your life. But there's lots about your life that's a mystery since you stopped living at home."

I tried to recall asking them the question about Rosie for the first time, but my mind was a blank. I wondered whether there were new holes in my head developing every hour. Was I in some kind of diminishing spiral of forgetfulness? Was my memory leaking out of me like oil from the elderly transmission in the Olds? It was probable. I knew that I'd have to think about it. If I didn't forget to.

THIRTEEN

THAT NIGHT, I slept with the damned dream again. It was like spending the night with an unwanted mistress, except that I hadn't gone sour on her, I'd never wanted her in the first place. Maybe I picked the wrong image, mistresses being somewhat out of my line. Still, maybe you get my meaning.

The dream had become a familiar obsession. Not only was it unwelcome, it was also boring. Nobody ever says or writes that about an obsession. Robert Louis Stevenson's Dr Jekyll had many emotions awakened when he turned into Mr Hyde, but he never spoke of boredom. He never said, "Oh, no! Not this boring old charade again!" Did Jack the Ripper mutter that to himself when he felt the urge for a stroll in Whitechapel? Was there an element of boredom mixed in with the release of sexual tension?

I knew that the dream probably held more clues for me, but I was still unable to decode them. Maybe solving this required a more intuitive kind of perception than I could provide. Introspection had never been my strong suit. I went over the details of the dream again in my head, while staring up at the irregularities in the ceiling and letting the curtain tracks carry me away from sense, logic, and deduction. My little grey cells had to do this, but they had to do it on their own. My memory had become like a sunspot. The act of looking at it burned it away in a flash.

Through the doorway, I could hear two nurses comparing holiday information. One was just back from the Islands, and the other was drinking in the news of the place.

"You got to get yourself some time back home, girl. Quality time, you hear? They still running cheap charters. No sense letting yourself grow strange, girl."

"Catch me getting on a plane these days! A woman can die of old age trying to get through Immigration." I let their voices drift out of sense, but allowed the silvery, keyboard sounds to wash over me as my mind went slack again.

When I next saw the light, it was electric and coming from my neighbour's overhead fluorescent tubes. I had been dreaming about Rose. She had come up the long flight of stairs leading to my office on St Andrew Street. I heard her knock at my door. A diffident knock. So many of my cases began with a knock like that. Rose came in. She was young and unsophisticated. Nervous, anyway; uncertain of herself calling on a private investigator. I got up from my chair, rounded the desk, and directed her to the chair facing my desk. I'd done this a million times and it was easy to imagine.

Where did we go from here? I thought. Clients usually began by telling me how they had come to select me from the short list of investigators in the Yellow Pages. "My doctor suggested you; my brother; my boss." Did Rose give me such a yarn? I couldn't come up with anything here that might help. And if it had to do with something criminal, why had she come to me and not to the police? Maybe it had to do with her love life. That was a good bet; most of my business has to do with love lives pushed out of shape or out the window. I fished with that promising bait for a few minutes and then discarded the notion. My Rose had her head screwed on solidly. She wasn't being jerked around by a gold digger or left pregnant with only dud promises to see her through to her due date.

Rose was taking shape in my mind, if not in reality. Rose had a problem, sure, but it wasn't her own. She was worried about somebody close to her. Her boyfriend? Her brother? Somebody she cared about but who wasn't looking after himself? She had a vulnerable friend, someone in danger. How far could I get trying to imagine my client? I couldn't even be sure there was a client. Still, lying there in bed, I knew she was becoming real to me. She had had grit enough to look up my name and address. She had weathered the steep climb to my door. Rosie wasn't just anybody; she was a force to reckon with. Rose was a client. *My* client!

Rose's problem brought me to Toronto, to the edge of the university campus. Toronto? If she lived in Toronto, why bother coming all the way to Grantham to knock on

my door? She might have come from Grantham, known
about me from Grantham, but Toronto was where the
problem was. Toronto was often the problem. Silver City
had a lot to answer for. Was my retainer that much cheaper
than Toronto PIs' rates? Unlikely. So, what did we have?
Rosie lives in Toronto, but hasn't done so for long; her
roots are still firmly in the soil of Grantham. She could be
a student. Maybe she lives in that residence. No, it's a
senior graduate student residence. My Rosie's an under-
graduate. But maybe her friend, the one she's worried
about, lives there. I made a note to get a list of the people
staying there.

The phone rang. I kept forgetting I had one. It never
occurred to me to make a call of my own. The very idea
of hunting for a name and number with my flawed brain
filled me with terror, but the relatively simple task of
finding the telephone instrument and lifting it to my ear
shouldn't have daunted me. I picked it up.

"Hello, Benny? Is that you?" I knew the voice at once.

"Martha!" It was Martha Tracy from Grantham. The
woman whose name I had been trying so hard to
remember.

"I'm glad you called! You can't know how good it is
to hear a voice from home."

"Hell, Benny, in your state you're happy to hear *any*
voice. That former layabout, your landlord, honked the
expensive horn on his Rolls at me while I was crossing
Queen Street. He put his head out the window to tell me
what had happened to you. But you know how Kogan

always gets things twisted, so I did my own digging. Got your pals in blue, Staziak and Savas, to add the icing. That's how I got your number. How are they treating you?"

It was a real delight to hear Martha again. She had helped me with one of my first cases, and ever since, I'd kept picking her brain whenever I got stuck. Martha was the true essence of Grantham: friendly, nosy, and comfortable. Kogan, my landlord, was a former panhandler who used to work the crowd shopping along St Andrew or Queen Streets. He was once a public eyesore. Now he was living proof that being lucky still beats out being enterprising. Hearing his name and Martha's voice suddenly made me want to see St Andrew Street again and feel the familiar pavement under my feet. But it all seemed so far away and so long ago.

"Benny? Are you still there or have they carted you off to the operating room?"

I grunted a response.

"What I mean to say is," she continued, "are you managing? Do you need anything? Because unless you need me bad, I'm going to open another bottle of beer. That's my formula for beating the hot weather. Okay?" I'd forgotten all about weather. It didn't exist here.

"It's good to talk to you, Martha. I've missed you. I need my Martha fix."

"*Now* you tell me! Where were you when I needed you?"

"Martha, you don't need anybody. You're an established institution."

"M'yeah. Don't let the bright paint fool you, Benny. I'm running short of durability. I've lost three drinking companions in seven months. If I *look* at somebody, she has to go into hospital; if I shake hands, she drops dead. People clear the room when they see me coming. I'm not counting your cop friends, Staziak and Savas. They told me straight out that they get danger pay when I turn up."

"How *are* they?" Staziak and Savas were the cops I got to do my detecting for me. I went to public school with Pete Staziak.

"They live under the threat of being forced to take up honest employment. They're aging fast. They told me your office was tossed by the crowd that tried to do you in. Is that right, Benny?"

"Martha, you're way ahead of me on that. I don't even know what my blood pressure is. Can't remember details any more."

"You always were more of an idea man than an encyclopedia. But really, Benny, is there anything I can do? Short of cooking and baking, that is. I don't run to canapés or chocolate cake. Try salted peanuts and I'm yours forever."

"Martha, I can't tell you how good it is to have you to talk to. Around here I get the 'Mr Cooperman' treatment, which gives me gas. There's such a thing as too much respect."

"M'yeah. I've had my share of that, too. Whenever I hear the word 'ma'am,' I look around for the arresting officer. The break-in at your office was in the paper. And your friend Staff-Sergeant Savas has one of his theories. But he won't tell anybody what it is until he's proven right."

I had always loved Martha's line of talk. She could strip the egotistical barnacles off the hulls of the worst of our politicians. I wish she would.

"Martha, did you get a call from my mother?" Two ideas were colliding in my head: one was about something Martha had just said, the other was why she had picked this moment to call me. Just then, one of the questions was lost.

"What?"

"You heard me. Have you talked to my mother?"

"Well ... yes. Seems to me she called. Just to keep me in the picture, you know?"

"Yeah, I know." My mother should be running the Secret Service. She's like an iceberg: you only see a small fraction of what's there."

"Benny? Did you hang up?"

"Martha, I've been trying to place a name."

"Hell, I do that all the time. Is that all that's bothering you?"

"It's the name of a local girl, I think. Someone with a connection to me and my job. It may be important. Could you spare it some thought?"

"Benny, I'll take a crack at anything. You know me. Are you going to tell me the name, or do you want to include that in the puzzle, too?"

"Sorry, Martha. I'm getting forgetful in my old age. The name is Rose. Or Rosie. Something like that."

"What's the last name?"

"Rose or Rosie is all I've got. There has to be a Grantham connection somewhere and a Toronto one."

"You know this isn't going to be easy?"

"That's why I asked you, Martha."

"Flattery'll get you everywhere, young man. Let me think: Rose or Rosie." Martha's talk broke down into internal rumblings, fragmented words, and phrases. I thought I could actually hear her teeth grinding at one point. The silence, such as it was, was a prolonged one, the sort that would make a calm man nervous. I held on, said nothing, believing that the best encouragement was my held breath. The first silence blended into a second, punctuated over the phone by noises of an indeterminate sort. Then:

"Benny, didn't you once cross swords with Stella Seco? She now calls herself Vanessa Moss in LA and Toronto. Thinks it sounds more professional. Remember, she had you jumping through hoops in Toronto for a few weeks last year?"

"Sure, I remember her. I'm still wearing the scars. What does she have to do with Rose?"

"She has a daughter with that name. Her father was a radio announcer. Paul. Paul Moss. His voice was so deep you got the bends from listening to him. Yes, their daughter was called Rose. She'd be in her early twenties. Did you ever meet her?"

"Stella would never have admitted to me or to anyone else that she had a grown-up daughter. That's not her style. If she's in her twenties, she could be in university.

Thanks, Martha, you just might have found the name I'm looking for."

"Well, it won't have been the first time. Benny, I'll talk to you again. My cigarettes are in the other room and I've smoked this one down to my knuckles. G'bye, you little devil. Keep in touch."

Stella Seco. I hadn't spared her much thought since I stopped working for her. As I told Martha, I still wore the scars from that job. She was a bloodless television executive whose houseguest had been murdered. For a while, the cops thought that she was the victim. Then they thought she was the murderer. Well, I helped sort that out. That case also took me up to Muskoka, the resort community a hundred miles north of here. I still dream about the little cottage Stella owns on the lake. At night, I sometimes get myself to sleep just by thinking of that place on the water.

For a few minutes, I stared at the hospital across the street. The wing in which I had been born was being demolished. It was making way for a newer idea of what a progressive hospital wing should be. From my present location on the fifth floor, and with heavy traffic running between us night and day, it was hard to miss the significance or the irony. But what could I do about it? I thought my mind could no longer deal with subtle things like irony.

Two of my therapists came looking for me. It seemed to me that they were always looking for me. One was for speech and the other was an occupational therapist. They wanted to know why I didn't love them any more, why I was ignoring my time scheduled with them. I tried to explain that I was diseased in the mind and that my memory had largely vanished. I could see that irony wasn't their first language, so I switched to an abject apology. They bought that conditionally, the condition being that I would make time to see them later in the day. I forget what the arrangement was, but it seemed to be a happy solution all around. I have a feeling that I've told you this already. I may have. The truth is that I can't remember.

When they had gone, I thought of all of the strings I was trying to manipulate from this hospital room. Anna was checking into my office, Martha had already come through for me, and maybe the Toronto cops would share more information before too long. In a peculiar way, I was sitting pretty. I was just trying on a big grin for size when a thought hit me from behind: everything was coming up roses, but where was Rosie? Had she come to see me? No. Not once in … in … how many weeks? If Rose was my client, where was she? Had she gone off to hire an investigator whose head wasn't mended with sticking plaster? Now it wasn't her presence that was bothering me, but her absence. And I couldn't see anything good coming of that.

I picked up the phone and dialled 411 and asked for the number of the office of Vanessa Moss, of the National Television Corporation, where Vanessa Moss worked. The operator did not play games with me. Without a quip or epigram, she passed along the main number. The next operator turned out to be the witty one. But I survived that and soon had Stella, sounding like her suspicious self, at the end of my ear.

"Benny Cooperman? I don't believe it! We have finished doing business together. The job I hired you for is over and paid for. A year ago! Thank you very much, and goodbye!"

"Wait a minute! Remember we grew up together. Remember Grantham Collegiate?"

"I've cut all my connections to Grantham, and your name was at the top of my list. We are no longer romping around at the collegiate. This isn't the Diana Sweets on St. Andrew Street. Now take my name out of your book. Get out of my life. If you think you've got an idea for a TV series, sell it to somebody else. You've got enough chutzpah for—"

"Both of us. I didn't call to rekindle old acquaintance, Stella. I'm not selling an idea for a sitcom. I don't want to do lunch. I want to talk about Rose."

"Rose? What about my daughter?" Her voice was different now, not quite unguarded, but I'd chipped through the enamel.

"When did you last talk to her?"

"Why, we … She is in summer school."

"Where?"

"Why, U of T. Here in Toronto."

"Is she living with you?"

"Of course not. She kept her room in residence. She didn't want to stay with me, and frankly, I didn't want her around. My life is all business, Benny. I didn't want to deal with …" She was protesting too much and she knew it. Like the television producer she was, she went on to "take two."

"I'm not the mothering sort, Benny. You know that. She has her own friends. She's in that new residence, the one that won all the architecture awards."

"Clarendon House? Under the O?" It was a guess, a leap in the dark.

"How did you know?"

"Because a professor was murdered there. I've *got* to talk to Rose. She may be in danger. Where is she?"

"Well, we had breakfast together, if you *must* know. We often do. As a matter of fact … As a matter of fact …" She stopped talking and that meant her twisted, scheming brain was working. "Benny, why are *you,* of all people, suddenly interested in my daughter?"

"Stella, the professor who was killed knew Rose. There may be a connection, and that means danger for Rose." I couldn't swear to that, but it seemed an inference worth cultivating. I didn't want to confess that Rose might be my missing client.

"What do you know about her? The dead professor? This is the first I've—"

"Stella, I—"

"Why do you always irritate me? You *know* my legal name is Vanessa Moss. Stella belongs to the buried past. You didn't question cheques with my preferred name on them."

I don't know why I kept hitting her with her discarded name. Maybe I was a bully at heart. Maybe because it was the only predictable hold I had on her. It kept alive the Grantham connection.

"Vanessa, please humour me. I need to find Rose."

"Why should I tell you, the most disloyal, argumentative, stubborn man on earth?"

"Because I'm interested enough to ask. Because you know it's not idle curiosity. Because you love your daughter. Because I might know something. Just *because*."

There was a pause as she looked for a loophole.

"Of course, I love my daughter," she finally said.

"What's her phone number then? Is she living alone?"

"Her permanent roommate is a medical student from Ottawa named Sheila Kerzon. Her father's a power in the Tory party. There's space for a third girl, but I don't know her." She gave me a number and I wrote it in my Memory Book.

"Thanks for the information, Stella."

"*What's going on,* Benny?"

"When I find out, I'll let you know. When you next hear from her, would you get her to call me?" I gave her my number, successfully reading it off the phone for the first time, and fell back exhausted. Stella always wore me out. Even in a short conversation, she could be a whole roomful of people. Her personality was part chameleon. Her saving grace was that little place she had in the woods up north. Nobody with a soft spot for the North could be entirely bad.

What did the conversation add up to? Rose is a resident under the O, where the dead professor came from.

Stella was not straightforward and clear about where Rose was right now. She hedged, she changed subjects. Up to her old tricks. Always looking for pits, never enjoying the olives....

When I woke up, it struck me that I hadn't been doing too badly. Martha's call, I think, had inspired the confidence to call Stella; that and a certain instinct for payback that lingered under my heart. I loved deflating her pretensions. I used to think I was bigger than that—above the need for petty revenge. But there it was, exposed for all to see: the real Cooperman, naked, mendacious, vindictive.

I punched my pillow and went back for another twenty minutes of dreamless sleep. I awoke suddenly when I remembered my appointment with my therapists. Grudgingly, I rolled out of bed.

I was walking on the treadmill when the mixture of body heat and mental free-ranging hit me with a thought: Stella, Rose's mother, had denied knowing about the death of Flora McAlpine in the Dumpster. But she called her "she," when I hadn't even hinted at the professor's sex.

FOURTEEN

THIS TIME WHEN I OPENED MY EYES, I slipped my feet out into the space between my bed and the window. The floor was chilly to the touch of my big toe. As I reached for my slippers with my left foot, I noticed that there was a piece of paper attached to one of them. I had mail! I was eager to inspect it, but I put it off until I'd made a phone call. I found the number in the phone book. It only took me ten minutes.

"Who is this?" It was the voice of a young woman.

"My name's Cooperman. I'm trying to reach Sheila Kerzon or Rose Moss. Can you help me?"

"They're not here."

"But they live there?"

"They don't come around very much. What do you want?"

"I'd like to talk to either one of them. Who am I speaking to, by the way?"

My belly had just started warming up with the anticipation of finally getting somewhere, when the line went dead. She'd hung up on me! I tried the number again. This time there was no answer. Disappointed, I turned back to the note attached to my slipper. It was from Anna. Who else? I sounded out each word until it came out like this:

Dear Benny,
You looked so sweet and peaceful lying there that I hadn't the heart to disturb you. I've gone for some coffee and I will drop back to have another look at you before heading back home. Slumber on,
Anna

In honour of Anna's imminent arrival, I gathered my washing things and closed the bathroom door behind me. All my trips to the bathroom were puzzling; my mind carried the ghost of a shower stall mounted in a bathtub, but it was nowhere to be seen. Rhymes With suggested that I was remembering the bathroom in the hospital I'd first been admitted to. Mount Sinai. This was the Rose of Sharon Rehab, where showers were scarcer. She was right, no doubt, but I felt the lack of a tub every time I went in there. The missing shower was like an amputee's phantom arm or leg; it belonged to an earlier period, which I was having difficulty mastering. The world didn't begin when I first looked up and saw Rhymes With's helpful face. The story of this crazy head of mine was longer than that. Why did I make it so hard to remember?

I took a run at my teeth, made a pass or two at my whiskers with the electric razor, and put on clean clothes. In fact, when Anna stood in the doorway, we both looked like we were ready for a stroll in the park. After Anna and Jerry had made small talk about the weather and the hospital food, we took a stroll down to the elevators by the nursing station.

Anna bought us both milkshakes in the café we'd visited before. Far enough from the traffic moving smartly along University Avenue, the café seemed like an oasis in a crowded desert.

"You haven't heard my big news," I said, pulling a straw from its paper sleeve. "You know I've had a name rattling around in my head?"

"Is *that* what makes the noise?"

"I'll ignore that. I've been haunted by the name Rose or Rosie for days. Now I know who she is. I think she hired me and that's what got all this started."

Anna breathed a quiet sigh. "Benny, should you be doing this?"

"They didn't stop us getting on the elevator."

"I don't mean *that*. I meant playing about with the business that put you here. If they wanted to kill you once, you're as good a target in your hospital bed as you were on the street. All that's needed is a bunch of flowers, and *anybody* can get in to see you."

"They keep a better watch than that. And statistically, very few attacks are committed on hospital patients."

"Statistically! You can prove utter nonsense with statistics. My colleagues do it all the time."

"Anna, I know you're worried about me, and I'm glad that it's you who's worried. But I'm in less danger now than I was at home. There, I was a walking target for anyone with a grudge against me. It was like that for years. You know that. At least now they have to buy some flowers before they can get to me. Don't worry. It's hard enough for the nurses to find me when they want me. Assassins will have to take their chances with the others."

"Funny your noticing that people worry about you. You didn't use to notice such things."

"It's not people, Anna, it's you. And I appreciate that. I always have. When we first met, you were worried that I might be ripping off your father."

"Everybody was always hoping to. I remember coming to your office and trying to psych you out."

"That was the first time I saw you. You were wearing blue jeans and came up to my office to annoy me."

"We actually met a couple of days earlier. You were talking to my father at our house."

"You seemed like a spoiled tomboy when you came to my office and started annoying me on purpose: peering over my shoulder to see what I was writing, looking at some private files. You made me angry. You made me very angry."

"You were no gentleman. You tossed me down the stairs."

"I ushered you to the door. I'm working in a tough business. What did you expect?"

"You threw me out! I was so mad, I could have strangled you."

In my mind's eye, I could see the Anna of those days: her absolute honesty, her hard, blazing, blue eyes, and later my difficulty breathing when I was near her. Now, across from me sat the same creature, undiminished by time and only driven halfway to the funny farm by this crazy life I'd been living. And it was crazy. How could one man tidy up all of Grantham? Even without the suburbs it was crazy. While I was here in the hospital, I should have the rest of my head examined.

"You gave me some sleepless nights, Anna."

"And you gave me my own share of long nights."

"You *knew* my life was hectic. You want an old lady who lives in a shoe!"

"I know. I know. There were good times too."

"And there will be more once I can get out of here. Let's get to my future. What did you find in my office?"

"Are you ready for this?"

"Shoot."

"Whoever hit you on the head has been to your office and has gutted your files."

"What?"

"The office has been trashed, Benny. I didn't want to tell you, but Frank Bushmill, your neighbour, found your door open and your files all over the floor. I'm sorry, darling."

I remembered that Martha Tracy had said something about my office. I'd been wondering whether my mother had put her up to calling me. The information about my office got lost in the mental shuffle. I can't keep two thoughts in my head at once any more. Imagine missing a break-in! In my own office! I really had a one-lane mind. Two ideas at the same time overloaded the circuits.

"Did you talk to Chris Savas about it?" I asked.

"I couldn't get through to him. I tried to, Benny. I'll keep at it."

"We have a very enterprising crook in this case, Anna. He murders ... Flavia? Fiona? I mean, Flora McAlpine on the campus of a major university, bumps me on the head here in Toronto, then drives to Grantham, where he guts my files. Very enterprising."

"Anybody who can strike here in Toronto and in Grantham is somebody you should be careful of, Benny. This villain cannot be trusted."

"It's still interesting."

"Well, 'interesting' may be *your* word for it. I think you should tell your Toronto police contacts what you remember now."

"Maybe it wouldn't hurt to rattle their chains with the news. And the Grantham police know about the break-in, even if they haven't yet tied it to the murder in the Dumpster here."

"You don't know that!"

"Sure I do. Frank Bushmill would have reported it. Frank's a good friend. By now, all the cops in the province know about it."

"You started to tell me about this Rose you've remembered," said Anna, bring me back on topic.

"Right, I was, wasn't I? Well, somewhere in this junk pile of a mind, I found the name Rose or Rosie. She's the daughter of Stella Seco. You remember Stella? Have I already told you this?"

"Don't worry. Keep going."

"Remember Stella Seco?"

"Who could forget her? She started building a career for herself before she was weaned. She was *All About Eve* and *The Little Foxes* all rolled into one attractive, but ticking, package."

"Well, now she's a big deal in television here in Toronto. Rosie's her daughter. Oh! I said that. After talking to Stella, I have a feeling that Rose has disappeared. A woman named Sheila Kerzon is her roommate. Both of them might be in danger. There may be a third student, but I don't know anything about her. Sheila's a young medical student from Ottawa, where her father's a power in the Tory party."

"So, why are you worried about Rose?"

"Because she hasn't been near me. How long have I been on University Avenue? First in one hospital, now in this one? Weeks? Months? And not a squeak from my client. She needed my help, brought me here to Toronto, and when I get hurt, she vanishes. Does that make sense? If she is okay, she'd have been in touch with me. If she's in danger, she may be hiding out someplace. In the light of what happened to that professor and me in the Dumpster, hiding out is the most optimistic possibility."

"All right, Rose has reasons for lying low. Besides you, who else is in danger?"

"*Danger?* That may be a little strong: more melodrama than hard facts." Anna nodded for me to keep going.

"Okay. Her roommates at Clarendon House. Home of the Dumpster. Depending on how much they know."

"In what way are they in trouble?"

"Well, they know at least as much as I do about all this. They may suspect where she's gone. I don't know. Maybe roommates don't talk to one another nowadays. The feeling I get back of my knees says that I should talk to her."

"But that's not much to hang an investigation on. Unless you're holding back on me."

"After talking to Stella, I have a feeling Rose has disappeared. It's a hunch, nothing I can take to the bank. Sheila Kerzon is her roommate. They live in the residence where Fiona or Flora McAlpine was living. So you see, she's as likely to get into trouble as I am."

"Is there anything more I can do?"

"You can try this number. See if you have better luck than I did." I gave her a crumpled copy of the phone number of the Moss/Kerzon residence.

"I'll try to find her next time I'm in town. Meanwhile, try to stay out of trouble for a change. And, Benny, remember what I said: this guy you're after is smarter than most crooks, and he has more resources. Promise me you'll be careful."

I promised, of course, and we finished our milkshakes like a couple of teenagers, seeing who could make their straw bark the loudest.

FIFTEEN

I TRIED TO WRESTLE all my separate confusions into one big ball and bounce it out the window. Of course, the window was closed. And my problems were not corporeal enough to allow themselves to be rolled up and tossed away.

I was on some villain's mind. On his *hate list*. He had put me in here, and he probably wasn't finished with me yet. Had the hospital security staff been told that my hide might be in danger? I pictured security guards sitting at a desk dozing off in front of a TV monitor. I saw a gang of black-robed, masked gunmen carrying a gigantic, horseshoe-shaped garland of red roses, like a victory wreath for a winning racehorse, pass the security desk. Perhaps getting helpful instructions on how to find my door from the least sleepy of the security guards. So much for daydreams coloured by too many Saturday afternoons at the Granada Theatre in Grantham.

Without thinking about it, I picked up the phone and called the number I had for Sykes and Boyd. I was startled to attention when I heard Sykes rasp out his familiar croak of response:

"Sykes."

"It's Ben Cooperman, Jack. I have to talk to you."

"They haven't sprung you from the Lame Brain Institute, have they?" I could always trust Sykes to be politically incorrect in private; he vetted his language in public.

"Maybe I got time off for good behaviour. Anyway, I was luckier than Flora McAlpine, wasn't I?" I enjoyed the pause that followed. I could almost hear the changing of gears.

"Oh, yeah. Sorry about that, Benny. We had to see how much you knew or remembered. Yeah, that was a damned shame about her. She was a terrific teacher, they say."

"You didn't honestly think I put her there and climbed in after her, did you?"

"Now, hold on, Benny. We go by the book: we check out all the angles. And we're still checking."

"Will the leaves have dropped from the trees before you move on to another suspect?"

"Come on, Benny! Let a guy do his job! Are you feeling any better?"

"Let's stay on the subject. I'll tell you about my sore head later. Was she hurt the same way I was?"

"Yes, she was, only her skull was crushed. Both of you went into the Dumpster at the same time. Are you sure you don't know her?"

"What am I going to use for a memory? As near as I can figure, she was a stranger. But I do have some kind of echo going around in my head. Let's say there's the ghost of a possibility. No more."

"In that case, Jim and I are going to try to come down to eat your chocolates. You got any of those boxes of fancy nuts?"

"Jack, I need to know about what the papers have said about my being beaned at the university residence. What's known about my condition?"

"Worried they might try again?"

"Sure. Wouldn't you be?"

"Benny, my boy, the *world* knows about your getting clobbered."

"That's only partly true. What's the rest of it?"

"What do you mean 'the rest of it'? What makes you think there's more?"

"It's in your voice. You should never have become a cop. Your voice gives you away."

"Okay. You're right. Whenever we have a material witness we want to keep under wraps, we tell the papers that the victim can't remember his own name. It's done to protect the witness. Now, as it happens in your case, what we said to the press was right on the money. You couldn't remember squat about what happened to you. So, we were only telling the truth to the press."

"Don't take any bows in public about that. It'll blow your game."

"I figured that angle, too. If they didn't believe us, you could be in a lot of trouble. I know that. I'll call the liaison man at the hospital and have them change your room."

"Yeah, to one with 'John Q. Public' or 'John Doe' on the door. Have you any idea how many people are trying to get a bed in here? The hospital people can't afford to play those games, Jack. They've got stretchers parked along the walls downstairs. What other good ideas have you had today?"

"We're still working out how the caramel filling gets inside the chocolate bar, Benny. There's lots of time. They told me you don't have to worry about rent until summer's nearly over. Try to look on the bright side."

"While I've got you on the line, tell me what the waiters from Barberian's told you about my car. You said it had been parked behind the restaurant."

"Yeah, Barberian's on Elm Street. A good place to go for a steak."

"Great! I'll remember that. Now, what did you learn?"

"Not much. One waiter remembered that it was pretty beat-up for a car belonging to one of their customers. How long *have* you been driving that thing?"

"Since the reconquest of the Sudan by Sir Herbert Kitchener in 1895 or whenever. Let's try to stay on the subject, okay?"

"Start by leaving dead generals out of this. Eliminate the irrelevant."

"Pachyderms aside, don't forget which of us has the brain injury. You been clobbered recently?"

"Okay."

"Unless you're interested in buying the car from me. They're getting scarce."

"*That* car? It should be in a landfill. The guy at our garage is still kidding me about it."

"What else do you have from the restaurant besides scullery gossip?"

"One of the busboys remembered that a man and a woman got out of the car. It's a small lot, takes maybe half a dozen cars, tops. The back door of the scullery, since you know the word, overlooks the lot. The woman was not much more than a girl, really. Much younger than he was. He didn't really get a good look at her. She *maybe* had fuzzy blond curls. He was dark with a moustache and dark glasses. But since nobody remembers seeing them in the restaurant, maybe the busboy was thinking of two other people."

"Or they walked right through and out the front door."

"Any way you like it, Benny."

"Thanks, Jack."

"Hey, are you really feeling better?"

"I can still tie my shoes and scrub my neck. They don't make me wear Depends at night. Why?"

"Oh, I'm just glad you're getting along."

"I'd feel a lot better if I knew who broke into my office in Grantham and went through my files."

"Yeah, we heard about that. Your pal Savas phoned me. Police work would be a lot easier if the hoodlums stayed within departmental boundaries. The way it is now, if a hoodlum is working in the next jurisdiction you might never hear about it."

"Yeah, I can think of a couple of examples."

I heard him sucking air through his teeth. At length, he added: "See you, Benny, so long. Keep your feet dry."

"Hey! One more question."

"What?"

"Last time we talked, you mentioned something about that college. I should have pressed you on that, but I didn't. What's going on over there?"

"Benny, you remember that movie *Chinatown*?"

"That's a long time ago. What about it?"

"In the movie, Chinatown in Los Angeles represents everything that is chaotic about this business, everything that doesn't play by the rules, that can't be figured or brought to book. For us here in this town, Simcoe College is Chinatown."

"Can't be as bad as that. They're just kids, after all."

"It's not just the kids, Benny. It's like *Chinatown,* I tell you."

"Hey! One more thing."

"Who do you think you are, Benny? Columbo? You're hounding me like I was a suspect."

"I need to tell you something. Something I think I've remembered. You want me to save it for later?"

"Okay, spill it."

"I was in Toronto working a case …"

"We figured that much. You're all finished at the dentist's."

"… and I think I may have been working for the daughter of Stella—You know her as Vanessa Moss."

"Her again! How does the daughter figure?"

"She's a student. She knows about me through her crazy mother. I may have come to Toronto to do some work for her."

"Since when are kids hiring private investigators? She give you a piece of her allowance?"

"My crystal's getting murky, Jack. I don't know more than what I've told you. Just remember I levelled with you."

"Sure, sure, sure. All I need are more clues from the Cracked Head Ward. See you." And he was gone.

I held on to the phone for a minute. The experience of phoning had been reborn in me. If I went at it fast and didn't think about it, I could call anybody.

Who was the girl in my car? The man was a car thief at least, but who was his companion? Was she there by choice or under duress? If the latter, it could have been Rose. Okay, why didn't she yell or run for it? Why did she play along? If the girl was part of the scam, then she might have been a witness to the murder, maybe an accessory. If Rose knew what had just happened to me and that poor professor, she wouldn't have gone along with the heavy without a murmur. Either this was a different woman or she didn't see me get clobbered. She trusted the guy at some point: she led me to him. Maybe he was about to get rid of her. I didn't like that.

Why would the staff allow anybody to park behind the restaurant and then walk out without ordering anything? Maybe they were good customers? Maybe the driver at least was well known to the maître d'?

I wandered down the hall looking for something to drink. My worries had brought on a thirst, and I could find only a juice dispenser that had run out of paper cups. The elevator down the corridor went *ping,* admitting new people to the floor. For the first time, but not the last, I wondered who they might be. I found a cup in my room and retraced my steps to the cooler. There I had a brief exchange with the former diplomat about the problems he was having in his end-game. While I nodded at what he said, only half listening, my mind went back to my conversation with Sykes. Why would my villain park his car behind a place where he or the girl were well known? Obviously, he wouldn't. But then, why not simply park the car on the street? After all, it was stolen. He could have left it anywhere. With me in the Dumpster, maybe dead or dying, the heavy had no reason to ditch the car right away. No doubt he had a car of his own somewhere nearby. But there was no reason I could see for bringing Barberian's Steak House into the plan at all. Unless it had something to do with the girl. It might have been part of the story he had been telling her.

So, what have we? Our villain was playing a double game. He was stringing the girl along, letting her think he had the run of the city, knew all the nifty places where he could park without paying, giving the impression of sophistication and mastery in small matters. All this to impress the girl? Maybe. Maybe it came as second nature to this particular villain. He liked to appear at ease in the big world. But what were the chances of his really knowing the restaurant? Slim. Very slim. He wouldn't take either her or his hot car anywhere near where he was known. That was enough reasoning for the moment.

From my position by the cooler, I could see into the dining room, where the diplomat was working his wheelchair close to a table by a window. He managed to remove the chair that was tucked under the table and slide his wheelchair into the spot it had occupied. He was getting good at manoeuvring that thing. The light filtering down on his face from the street gave a smoothing effect to his weathered features. The tableau of the old man by the window reminded me of one of those Dutch paintings you see in museums.

"Mr Cooperman?"

I turned to see a new and unfamiliar face. He stood over six feet tall, was reed-thin, and wore his long mouse-coloured hair in a ponytail. He told me his name, which I promptly filed in my list of forgotten names. I smiled back at him and, encouraged, he went on to explain that he was a social worker attached to my case. He led me into his office, which was just across the hall. (Did he lie in wait here, like a spider waiting for its prey, and then leap out at victims as they passed?) When we were seated in his tiny office, he reviewed my file, which he had attached to a clipboard. The books on his walls were those of his profession.

"You're making good progress here, Mr Cooperman."

"What else have I got to do? When are you going to let me go home?"

"Ha! Most people want to know how long they can stay. Are you in a hurry to leave us?"

"Mr —, I'm sorry, I can't hold on to names any more."

"Martin. Stan Martin."

"Well, Mr Martin, I can't run my life from a hospital bed. Do you know how long it's going to be?"

"You've got a long way to go before we can start thinking of your release date."

"Is this a hospital or a parole board? I don't *believe* this!"

"What floor are we on?"

"What?"

"What floor? *This* floor. What's its number?"

"What's that matter? The fifth or tenth. I don't know."

"You don't know because numbers, figures, confuse you. They don't stay in your mind any more. That's why you were given a Memory Book."

"Oh, you were in on that?"

"That's no secret. Standard practice. Everybody with your sort of injury gets a Memory Book. I hope you didn't think you were our test case?"

"Maybe I did. Even in hell, some people think they're special."

He looked at me for a long minute, trying to find my baseline, I guess, then picked up his papers again. "Your memory is still a problem. It's going to get better, but it isn't better yet, is it? Do numbers or names confuse you more? Do you remember my name? Any of your nurses' names? What about your therapists? Or should we switch to street names? Does Yonge Street cross

Bloor? Does Bloor cross St George? Does St George cross St Clair?"

"That's a cheap shot and you *know* it. You *know* I don't live in Toronto. I … I … Okay, I'll concede: I have a way to go."

"Good. We want to work with you, Mr Cooperman. We want to put you back in touch with what you've lost. As far as possible. We have some useful stratagems, based on a few years' practice." He paused for a moment, reading from the clipboard balanced on his knee. "Have you noticed yourself confusing ordinary, everyday objects?"

"That clipboard must tell you that I do. Yes, I confess. I've stood in front of the toilet with my toothbrush poised and I've addressed the sink in a similarly inappropriate way. But my slate's clear on the oranges–and–apples charge. I haven't seen any, so I couldn't confuse them." I was beginning to sound like Captain Queeg in *The Caine Mutiny*. All I needed was a couple of ball bearings.

He nodded sagely in the manner of all medical and paramedical people. "Why haven't you been doing your therapy, Mr C? There are three therapists waiting for you every morning."

"The Ghost of Christmas Past and his two friends?"

"Why aren't you going down to the gym, Mr Cooperman?"

"Until a little while ago, I didn't know you had one. Do you have a pool as well?"

"Not what *you'd* call a pool, Mr Cooperman. A pool for special needs."

"Damn it! You guys have a tidy phrase to cover everything! This isn't a conversation, it's a rub-down with feathers."

"Just stop beating your skull against the wall. You've had a bang on the head. You've had memory loss. Your life is going to be different from now on. Those are facts. We can't change them. It's time to get used to the facts and begin the return journey. We can't take you all the way, but we can give you a start. Okay?"

"Okay," I said. "Let's make a start."

"The gym's a good place to get your muscle tone back, Mr Cooperman. Try it out; you'll be glad you did."

"Thanks."

" Where do you stand on OT?"

"Sorry. What's OT?"

"Occupational therapy. They work with you, helping to create strategies for making your life easier. That's where you work out practical solutions to solve your problems. We had a patient who could never recognize his own toothbrush in a glass with the brushes belonging to the others in his family. We got him one with a white dot on the handle. Not all strategies are as simple as that, but most of them are. The people at OT have met difficulties similar to yours, so they can anticipate some of your problems."

"Sounds like I'm going back to school."

"Would you like to get back to Grantham?"

"As fast as possible."

"But you have family here, too, don't you?"

"Sam, my brother, works here. My parents come into Toronto to see me when they can. I don't know what I want, except to get out of here as quickly as possible."

"They are not admitting new patients in Grantham General—we checked—because beds are scarce there too. The best strategy for you is to keep going to your classes—speech, OT, and gym. That's the fastest road out of here, Mr Cooperman."

"Fine. What can I do to help get myself in shape?"

"Just keep going to your regular classes every day."

"I'll try to do that. Tell me, is there any restricted access for visitors who might want to see me? Are some visitors being turned back by the desk or downstairs?"

"Dr Cooperman has given us a list of suitable visitors. Want to see it?" He turned his clipboard around so that I could look. Seeing what was written there was another matter, which the social worker quickly recognized. He turned it around again and soon had rhymed off the names of the people I could remember seeing, going back for as long as I could remember: yesterday. Just before he put the clipboard away, I got him to add a few names:

Bill Brewer, Harry Hawk,
Old Uncle Tom Cobbley and all,
Old Uncle Tom Cobbley and all.

He did this without blinking.

SIXTEEN

THE SOCIAL WORKER TOOK ME DOWN a few flights in the south elevator to the gym. There, he introduced me to the woman in charge, someone I vaguely remembered by the colourful turns of phrase she used. Generally, I avoided strenuous exercise when I could, but I looked forward to my classes with What's-her-name.

I think I've already described the gym. If I haven't, it was like most gyms: tall-ceilinged, sweaty, and full of people rolling on mats or pedalling stationary bikes. The patients concentrated on moving weights from one level to another, walking up and down short flights of steps, and raising their stricken limbs as far as they could.

"You get yourself together and bring your carcass down here tomorrow after breakfast. How does that grab you?"

"If I'm not snagged on the end of somebody's needle."

"We can throw a gaff at you just as easily down here, Mr Cooperman. It's part of our training. I'll send some-body to collect you."

"Great!"

I both liked and disliked the idea of being collected. It was a boost to my ego to be important enough for them to send a conductor after me, and at the same time, I was sad to see that I required so much looking after. Sometimes I could go for ten or fifteen minutes without running into one of my newly acquired infirmities. The next minute, I was tripping over them whatever I did. I was like a prisoner running to the end of his tether.

The next morning I woke up to something completely different.

"Mr Cooperman?" It was the voice of a well-dressed young woman, as I saw when I rolled over in my bed, my refuge from the world.

"So, you want urine or blood? Today you're in luck: I've got both in stock." I was getting used to these assaults, even though I half-guessed that this was no doctor, nurse, or social worker. I was having her on.

"Neither. I'm not a nurse or doctor."

"Well, that's a relief. A novelty! How can I repay your indifference to my unique homemade vital fluids? Half of my kingdom? The whole thing? Well, take it, and the best of British luck to you."

"I'm Sheila Kerzon." The name sounded familiar. I knew I'd heard it recently. Her expression gave me the message that the name would mean something to me. I glanced at my Memory Book. After some page turning I was able to decipher her name.

I couldn't disguise the sudden intake of air that made no secret of my surprise. She didn't seem to notice the time delay. To meet someone neither related to me nor with a professional concern for my health was in itself a novelty. To meet someone who was attached to the world beyond the constant chirping of the elevator and the slow padding of stroke victims up and down the corridor was a delight I can hardly describe. To be suddenly in the presence of someone I had been thinking of for the last few days was like touching earth after a journey in space. She was part of that *real* world I had been sequestered from. She was looking at me as though she'd rather be in Philadelphia.

"Are you all right?" I asked. A funny question coming from a hospital bed. I sat up carefully, like I was made of spun glass, throwing my stockinged feet to the floor.

"Sure," she said, then noticing my roommate working on his stamp collection in the other part of the room, she asked, "Is there some place we can talk?"

Jerry made a gesture that suggested that he was about to leave, and I grabbed my dressing gown and slippers. I grinned at Jerry, who didn't like to stutter before strangers.

"It's okay, Jerry. A change of scene will do me good." In the end, after a lot of "After you, my dear Alphonse," we made for a small study next to the dining room. The distant smell of stale tobacco spoke of a more indulgent era. I took a chair near the window, so that the light through the pane would illuminate my visitor's face.

Sheila was a pretty little thing, with big brown eyes that commanded and got attention. She was casually dressed, neither stylish nor student-like. Her skirt and sweater were black and she carried a dark cardigan. She wasn't very tall, about my height, and her short skirt helped to show off her long legs. This served to distract me from seeing at once that her two upper front teeth were not her own. It was a good job, but in the bright glare they didn't reflect the light like her own teeth did. In another setting, I might not have noticed. Her hair hung darkly, with the sunlight finding and showing off the highlights. I could see that she looked after herself. Both of her ears had been pierced for multiple studs—and there might have been another on a nostril— but her only ornament was an expensive wristwatch.

There was the usual awkward pause, after which I asked, "You're Rose Moss's roommate, right?"

"Well, yes. I am or I *was*. I don't know. I've still got all of her stuff. Her mother hasn't picked it up yet. Hoping for the best, I guess. Do *you* know where she is, Mr Cooperman?"

"No. She hasn't contacted me. She may not know where to find me. Is it common knowledge that I'm in here? I haven't seen the papers," I said, not telling her why.

"It was on TV and on the radio. About your losing your memory and all. You don't look like you've lost your memory."

"What does *that* look like?" I suppressed further comment, noting that my ego was unusually thin-skinned. She was blushing and examining the carpet. Why do I sound off like that? She pulled out a clean handkerchief and blew her nose.

"I'm sorry," I said lamely. "I'm going stir-crazy in here."

"No, *I'm* sorry for being insensitive. I came to see you because I need your help. I've been trying to find Rosie and I can't. Will you help me? You were helping her. She told me."

"Look, I'm in no shape to help *anybody*. I get winded tying my shoelaces; I can't keep three things straight in my mind at once. You'd be better off talking to the cops about this. Pete Staziak and Chris Savas."

"I've talked to Staff-Sergeant Sykes."

"Good. *He's* the guy. Forget about Staziak and Savas. They're in *Grantham,* where I live." Once again my acquired idiocy was catching up with me: I still couldn't remember where I was. My stomach groaned like a stalled car's reluctant ignition.

"You *see*? My head's still not functioning. I forgot. That's why I'm on sick leave from my work. My mind doesn't have a bookmark in it. I'm not even dead certain that I was working for your roommate. I don't know anything for sure. Do you know why I was helping her?"

"Something to do with one of her professors: Dr Herbert Haddow."

At last I had a name! "I suspected that she might be involved with one of her teachers."

"Not quite her style, Mr Cooperman. But what if something has happened to Rose?"

"If anything has happened to your friend, it probably happened around the same time I was attacked, and that was months ago."

"So, you're going to just walk away from her?"

"Listen, please. I'm not up to a real job. I don't have the sap left in me. Maybe next year this time, I'll be stronger. I may even be able to remember what happened two days running."

"That'll be too late."

"It's too late for me, Sheila. Don't you see?"

"Will you ever recover your memory?"

"When I ask that question, my doctor asks me whether I'm getting enough exercise. I don't think they know."

She nodded slowly, showing she understood. But I couldn't leave it at that.

"You see, I wouldn't know where to start. Even if I could get out of here. Besides, I don't even know for sure that I was working for your friend. Or if I was, how long I'd been doing it."

"But you *have* to help me. There's no one else."

"How many ways do you want me to say it? Hell, I don't know what she looks like. *Or* that crazy professor of hers."

"She's small, pretty, and with enough teeth for both of them. Have you changed your mind?" There was a forlorn hope in her eyes.

I shook my head.

"The Yellow Pages are full of private investigators who don't fall asleep every twenty minutes and who can remember names. Before this happened to me, I'd have been your man, but not now. I'm not any good."

She looked stricken. I held the door for her and we walked to the elevator. I tried not to look at her directly.

She didn't meet my eyes then either. The ping of the elevator announced the end of this awkwardness.

I continued our conversation in my head as I walked back to the room. More reasons came to mind why I couldn't help her. I stretched out on the bed, feeling like a malingerer. "I'm sorry," I said to her in my imagination. "You can get far better help than I can offer you." The imaginary Sheila nodded, clenching her teeth. I thought of myself working the investigation with my mind like Swiss cheese. Finally cornering my leading suspect, I'd announce to the world that the guilty person was What's-his-name!

"You look down in the mouth, Mr Cooperman, like a man who's just had to put down the family cat." It was, Rhymes With. I rolled over in her direction. She looked crisp in her uniform, but soft and friendly too.

"Hi," I said. "I just had a visitor."

"I saw her. She looked mighty peeved about something when she left. What did you say to her, Mr C?"

"I told her I couldn't help her with her problems because I was hanging around this place."

"You told her the truth. You can't help yourself out in the street." She brushed a strand of hair from her eyes and let her fingers tidy it without looking. "You wouldn't be much of a help to anybody else that I can see. You're still recovering, man. No, you've got to work at getting out of here by going down to the gym. Your therapist was up here looking for you."

"I forgot."

"I know. I know. I hear that a hundred times a day. It's endemic. Why don't you take your cute butt down to the gym and surprise her?" Her smile returned as she looked down at me.

"I will. *I will.*"

"Mr C, that was the woman who was here before. She said she was your wife."

"My wife? But I've never even been engaged!"

"Well, you tell her. She's been here to see you before."

"She was probably afraid you wouldn't let her in if she wasn't kin of some kind. Did she call herself Mrs Cooperman this time too?"

"I don't know. I wasn't on the desk. Ask them." She backed away, giving me a parting toss of her head to show me that things weren't that bad after all.

I made my way down to the gym on my own. I took the elevator at the far end of the corridor. It seemed simpler than the last time, less confusion about the floor number I was aiming for. For about forty minutes I climbed stairs, walked a treadmill, and rode a stationary bike that presented simulated hills to me as I pedalled. The woman in charge gave me verbal support from time to time. She had a pleasant way of speaking. It was original and colourful. She said she came from Hamilton. That was the best thing I'd ever heard about that place.

Afterwards, I felt like a shower, but I felt unequal to the task. I settled for a lie-down on my freshly changed bed. I was surprised how quickly I was asleep.

SEVENTEEN

THE LIGHT THAT CAME THROUGH my window pitched the same shapes on the curtains, and the same footsteps and wheels ran along the hallway. The same high-pitched arpeggios of Island laughter rang outside my door, announcing another ordinary day here at the rehab. The day got off to a bad start, however, when I tried to brush my teeth with hair cream. It was the sort of day when I'd be sure to mistake apples and oranges and, if I were on the outside, try to put my leftovers in the dishwasher and the dirty cups in the fridge.

Then it got worse. A letter arrived addressed to me here at the hospital. I didn't know its contents until Anna breezed in from who knows where and read it to me.

Its strident and bullying tone seemed out of place in this healing environment:

Dear Mr Cooperman,
It has come to our attention that you have been
pursuing your private business on the property of Simcoe

College, that you have been doing so without sanction or permission from the governing body of the College, and that you have been a source of upset and disruption to both the students and the faculty alike. If you have legitimate business that brings you to this college, you must make the nature of your business known to the Board of Syndics before being allowed to have access to the students in our care. Your compliance with this request is imperative, and any further breach of our rules will be dealt with by our legal advisers. A copy of this letter is being sent to the body governing the licensing of private investigators in the Province of Ontario at Queen's Park.

Yours sincerely,
George W. Nesbitt

"*Well,* Benny, you've been told off in no uncertain terms and threatened to boot."

"I don't like the sound of that."

The tone of the letter chipped away at my exaggerated opinion of higher education.

Who was this George W. Nesbitt? Was he an academic, a university cop, or what? And how many people over there knew what happened to me or where to find me? That girl, the one who came to see me, *she* knew where. Well, I guess I'm still visible. I began to wonder how many people I had questioned when I was last on the campus. It couldn't have been very many. Students don't usually complain to the university cops about things like that. Or at least I didn't think they did. I thought that they were more worried about old geezers trying to pick up young women and luring them away from the hard chairs in the library to the comfort of a hotel-room mattress.

The letter excited my heart rate, as my nurse informed me, as she checked my oil and gas. I wanted to march down there and find out what was going on and see that it was written up and printed on every front page from St John's to Victoria. The nerve and the gall!

"Don't let this creep upset you, Benny. I see a frightened bureaucrat behind that letter. I don't think it's much more than that. It's rude and bullying, not up to the university's high standards. I wouldn't lose any sleep over it. When the university's heavy artillery comes after you, it won't start with a popgun like that."

"I wasn't planning to trespass on their sacred turf again. I wouldn't know where to start or whom I'd talked to already. It's too complicated."

"Yes, I know. But listen, my dear heart, wasn't your trip to the campus some time ago?"

"Months."

"Then why are the university people contacting you now?"

"I *have* made a few phone calls. I've talked to a few people."

"True …"

"Maybe somebody on the campus is stirring things up. That's a guess. If there is some bottom to all of this, if the girl was mixed up in something serious, then the university partly and the college definitely will suffer from any bad publicity. I wish I could go over there!"

"Would you like me to see this Sheila person you told me about? I'm going to be there this afternoon."

"I was just talking to her. Was that yesterday? She came here, asking for help, and I sent her away."

"That couldn't have been easy for you."

"Yeah. And there was something else. But I can't put a name to it yet. Perhaps you could try to explain to her why I can't take on the search for her missing roommate. And see if you can get any names or details of what's going on over there. Sheila did tell me something about a professor. You should be able to dig up something, especially if Rose is truly missing."

"Missing to you, to me, Benny; missing to Sheila Kerzon, but not yet missing officially to the likes of George W. Nesbitt. If it makes you any happier, my dear, the letter bothers me too. It's officious in the extreme. It's like giving the third degree to someone who reports that the plumbing isn't working in the third-floor loo of the engineers' residence. It's energy spent in the wrong direction."

"There's a lot of that around these days. And stop hanging around those pimply, beer-swilling engineers. They're jailbait, professor."

"I have to keep reminding myself. But they are *so* healthy!"

"Good health in the young is a notorious device for disarming vigilance in horny female professors. I read that somewhere."

"You aren't thinking of renewing your lease with me, are you?"

"I could be. I could be thinking of making an offer. You never know. I can't remember what I'm missing."

"You didn't get hit on the head *that* hard."

"Come and rub the bump through which my youth escaped."

"Benny!" She looked genuinely shocked. I tried to review what I'd just said, but for the moment, it was gone. Then the context returned with a ding.

"I mean my *head,* idiot!"

"Sure you did." She began to gather her things together. "Bye, now."

"Hey, you look out for yourself, okay?" I had a sudden vision of Anna being dropped into the Dumpster.

"I always have. I'll see what I can find out about that fellow with the initial."

"George W. Nesbitt. I'm writing it down. The *W* stands for warthog."

"Or Want-wit. I'll call later. G'bye!" Her kiss was more than a perfunctory peck, I am glad to say. Something to remember.

In my shattered memory, dinner that night gave me a lift. I felt like a grown-up for the first time in a long while. The meal was indifferent—well-done roast beef, or maybe lamb or turkey, and green peas that alternated hard and soft centres. The diplomat was sitting to my right, my roommate opposite, and one of the remaining gourmets— one had been discharged—next to him. I had forgotten all of their names.

"The situation in the Middle East is extremely dangerous just now," said the gourmet.

"When has it been anything else?" demanded the diplomat.

"I've never had a bad meal in Tel Aviv."

"I've never had a *good* one. But that's the diplomatic curse. They try so hard and they always fail. It's like the rubber chicken you get in American hotel dining rooms."

"And Canadian!"

"And English!"

"No! I protest that I have eaten very well in London and in some of the big hotels."

"Read your Orwell. You were lucky."

"I don't think so. I think English food has improved over the years. The prices are terrible, but the food *is* better."

And so on. At the end of the meal, I was feeling both well fed and superior. I felt like ordering brandy for everybody and offering cigars around. Smoking was not allowed and the brandy was unobtainable, but the conversation had lifted the spirits even if we were not allowed to partake of any.

It was at least an hour after dinner before I heard from Anna. I had all but given up on her and was feeling peevish and unloved, when the call came. I checked my watch for the first time in weeks: it was seven-thirty.

"Benny! Are you still there?"

"Sure. I was just experiencing a sensation of relief. I had started wondering whether to look for you in a Dumpster somewhere."

"That's not funny, but thanks for the thought. I'm okay. I did some nosing around, as you like to say, asking about your Professor Haddow."

I tried to remember who Haddow was; then the name began to resonate: he was the professor Rose was interested in. The one she came to see me about, if I've got that straight. But when did I tell Anna about him? That I never did get straight.

"Professor Haddow? Yes? Did you talk to him?"

"Forget about him. He's long gone from here, Benny. Old enough to have been in World War II. Retired. He can't be your man."

"But Sheila Kurzon said ... Why would she...?" I tried to think through our conversation at double speed. Brains should work like recording machines. When I didn't get anywhere after a minute, I shrugged and took a breath. "Okay. Exit Professor Haddow. What else did you get?"

"That's my news! Rosie Moss had a campus ... *beau*— that's too old-fashioned. 'Boyfriend' is too public. You know what I mean. An older man. An extracurricular interest. He's a lecturer in biochemistry, one of her instructors. A nice guy from all reports. Good-looking and an inspired teacher. But here's the thing. He was slipping in his work last term. He even failed to meet some of his classes. That's a serious no-no around any university, Benny. And now he's gone missing too."

"Vanished? Just like that? Well, I'll be damned!"

"And I couldn't find your friend anywhere. Sheila Kerzon."

"Then how do you know about Rose and the professor?"

"I talked to several of the summer school students in a campus café, the Tuck Shop. It's very twee and crumpets. A hangout for undergraduates. They *all* said the same thing. It's *synoptic*, Benny. I've got Matthew, Mark, and Luke on this."

"Forget the Gospels for a minute. Do we know this young fellow's name?"

"I'm sorry. I keep forgetting about your poor memory. He's Dr Steven, with a *V*, Mapesbury. He has a degree from Exeter College, Cambridge, which means that he came to us with impressive credentials."

"I thought Exeter was a prep school for the wealthy."

"See how wrong you can be. This Exeter is covered in very old ivy. You can take my word for it."

"The last time I trusted anyone about ivy, it turned out to be Virginia creeper. So don't mess about with me, woman."

"Your man has a good reputation. He's been around for the last five years. He may have put down roots. You can check that in the phone book. Can't be too many Mapesburys. He's a good teacher, from all accounts, and very popular with the kids."

"Will you be here tomorrow?"

"Nope. I'll be back on Thursday. Good hunting."

There only was one listing for Mapesbury in the Toronto book. It took me some minutes to locate it, because for a while I was searching for it under *W*. I've been looking for a theme to my war with the alphabet, but I haven't found it yet.

"Mapesbury, S. P." It could be an estranged wife or it could be a dead end of another sort. I tried out my fingers on the phone without allowing myself time to brood about it.

"Hello?" It was the voice of a little girl or boy.

"Is your mother or father there?"

"My mother's here, but I thought *you* were going to be Daddy because it's my birthday today." I decided that it wasn't a little boy. Little girls take pains to sound grown-up on the phone. Little boys are less interested.

"Well! A very happy birthday from me to you. I hope you get what you're hoping for."

"I hope that Daddy remembers."

"Could you let me speak to your mother?" The kid was breaking my heart. She left the line without speaking again and I could hear the sound of a far-off conversation, then the approach of footsteps.

"Hello? Who is this, please?"

"My name is Cooperman. Ben Cooperman. I'm looking for Steven Mapesbury. Can you help me?"

"Ha! If you're looking for my scapegrace husband, you'd better join the queue. He's becoming the most popular missing man of the year."

"When did you last see him?"

"Not counting nightmares, I haven't seen him for months. Not since Good Friday."

"I'm sorry," I said, not knowing what else to say.

"So am I. So are the children. We are all sorry and doesn't being sorry make all the difference?" She was using a portion of bitterness to cloud the painful absence. The mother was made out of the same stuff the daughter was. I had to pinch my nose to go on talking. Only, she started first.

"May I ask to whom I'm speaking? I didn't catch your name when I came on the line and Dympna didn't catch it either."

"My name is Cooperman. Ben Cooperman. Did I tell you I'm a private investigator? I'm trying to find your husband as a way of finding another person who has also gone missing."

"Seems as though quite a gang of them have gone off."

"Yes, it does."

"You're not the police, then?"

"No. I'm a private investigator. I'm from out of town. You have no idea where your husband may have gone? Is there a cottage or relative?"

"No. Why are you asking me the same questions the others did? I wish someone would just tell me whether he's alive or dead."

"I'm not trying to make trouble for anybody, but I need information. Who, for instance, are his university friends? When did you see him last? That might be a place to begin."

"Isn't this duplicating the work the police have already started? I was asked these same questions months ago! Are you all stirring the same pot? I'm sorry. As you may understand, I've been living under some stress. I wasn't educated to the stiff upper lip."

"I'm sure you're right, but the cops won't let me look over their shoulders. I have to do my own digging."

"Why you? What do you get out of it?"

"My sanity, for a start. It's a long tedious story. I'd rather not go into it on the phone. But, believe me, I'm not out to hurt anybody."

"There's so much to tell."

"And you've told this to the police?"

"Months ago. I mean, my God, the man's been gone since Good Friday! Something serious has happened to him. He might be dead."

"I doubt it. There aren't too many unreported homicides in Toronto. I think it's unlikely that he has met with anything as serious as you're suggesting. But I don't know. Was he mixed up in anything irregular on campus? Something dubious? That could have a bearing."

"He was up to something, I think. But I don't know what it was. Wives don't always know these things. A year ago we were struggling to make ends meet; now we're quite comfortable. I've even paid for a new TV."

"Did your husband tell you where the money came from?"

"No, but if you like, you could come around and I could give you a drink while you ask your questions. Is that how you private people do it?"

"Sorry. I can't. I'm stuck here and I can't get away."

"You sound as if you're in jail or in hospital with your leg in one of those traction things."

"You're not far off the mark. Can you tell me what the college people you've talked to have said?"

"Mostly, they've said, 'Leave it to us; we're on top of things.'"

"Who were you talking to?"

"A professor named Nesbitt. I didn't get his full name."

"Can you give me the names of a few of your husband's university friends?"

"Let's see: there's Morgan Bett. He's a friend from our early days in Toronto. He's retired now, but he comes in on Monday to have coffee with the other retired professors. That's in St Gabriel's Hall, on St George Street. He's building a mad tower from discarded gravestones up north someplace, but he comes in regularly to meet with the boys."

"Anyone else?"

"Well, there's Boolie. He's a demonstrator and lab technician."

"Boolie?"

"Abul Khair Moussuf. He's Kashmiri. But he's a naturalized Canadian. And then there's Parker Samson, *Dr* Parker Samson. They call him *Gauche*. An old football nickname. He's the senior man in biochemistry. He calls from time to time, asking whether I've heard from Steve. He's a good friend of my husband's, helped us to get this place. He was always trying to help Steve out. You could start with him." I thought she was going to give me another name, but she had stopped, as if she was thinking about what she had said so far. At last she continued, "That's all I can think of right now. My mind isn't working very efficiently."

"You forgot to give me one name."

"*Did* I? Which one?"

"Your own. I should add it to my list."

"It's Laura, if you must know. I've had the baby down with croup all week. Give me your number and I'll call you if I remember anything else."

"Just to make sure: you've not had any contact, either directly or indirectly, with Steve, right?"

"That's right."

"How well do you know this Professor Samson?"

"Ever since we arrived here. He helped Steve through the red tape at the university. He's been a good friend."

"And Boolie?"

"Again, another good friend. Except that Boolie's younger and not as high on the ladder as Dr Samson."

"Oh, one last thing: I just want to get this straight in my head. Dympna has just had a birthday. How old is she now?"

"Didn't I tell you that? She's four. And her sister, Clea, will be two in December. Anything more? Do you think that they'll ever find my husband? I'm running out of things to tell the children."

"Mrs …" Here I coughed to cover up the name that had escaped my mind. "I don't know what to say and whatever I said, it would be a guess. I just don't know enough. By the way, what does he look like?"

"He's not very tall, but he doesn't seem to be a little man. Maybe it's his golden curls. He used to be quite cherubic, really. He looks like one of those winged cherubs in the corners of ancient maps. And in Italian paintings. Putti, or whatever they are called. Yes, he looks like an aging putto. His cheeks aren't quite rosy any more, but his face remains chubby. Oh, and I mustn't forget! He lost a front tooth!"

"When was that?"

"He told me that it died when he was still an under-graduate—long before I met him in England. He'd had an implant done in London. It looked very natural. Steve boasted that the dentist had done one of Elizabeth Taylor's front teeth. He did all the top film stars. Of course, Steve got a good price because they were at school together. Anyway, when I saw him last, the tooth had broken off leaving a gold wire sticking out. I bent it double so he wouldn't snag his tongue. He told me he'd been hit playing hand ball, but in the light of what's happened since …"

"I see what you mean. You checked his story?"

"Not at once, but after he went missing I did. He hadn't been playing with any of his usual partners for weeks."

"You'd make a good private eye."

"I used to write business reports for a company in Soho. It helped earn a little money for food and my music lessons. We checked out the credit rating of small businesses around the world, then sent back reports that the K. M. Batcheles Co. was a man outside Meerut, India, with an old Remington typewriter under a palm tree." We laughed a little.

"One last thing: do you know the name Flora McAlpine?"

She thought a moment and repeated the name aloud to herself. "I'm sorry. I can't make a connection. Was she one of Steven's things?"

"Things?"

"*You* know, episodes, girlfriends, bits of fluff."

"The only thing I know about her is that she's dead."

"Oh! I'm sorry. It's hard to remember sometimes that this isn't just about us. I should know better."

"Thanks. Anything else? I have a description."

"He looked a perfect fright: a cherub with a missing front tooth; Bugs Bunny with a missing incisor."

"You've been a big help. I'll be in touch. Give Dympna my best wishes on her birthday."

I disconnected, after giving her my number at the hospital. Laura was a vivid character, even over the phone. Like Stella, but without her bite I added her name and the others to my Memory Book. Then I went looking for a cup of coffee to sustain me until the next meal. As I poured it, I thought of little Dympna, her sister, and their absent father.

EIGHTEEN

WHEN I RETURNED TO MY ROOM from the gym the next day, still damp with perspiration, I called Professor Samson first and bombed out. His machine told me that he was going to be busy with meetings all day. The university didn't have an office number for A. K. Moussuf. The numbers I got for him were all outdated and the people I talked to didn't have his current number, but they were all sure that he was still somewhere around the scientific end of the university.

The third man on my list, Morgan Bett, could be found on Friday at the St Gabriel's Hall on St George Street. I wondered how I could find him. I imagined going to the campus on my own, bursting in on a gaggle of young, bushy-tailed professors, all staring at me in their black gowns and mortarboards. I didn't think I'd last very long, and my inquiries would be doomed. But there was something about the drama of the thing that attracted me, and while I was saying, "No, no, it's a bad idea," I found myself climbing into my underwear, followed by my trousers, shirt, jacket, and tie.

I made it down the elevators without seeing a lifted eyebrow and was in the street before I knew what I was doing. The heat hit me first. The pavement was like a gridiron or barbecue. I'd dressed for the familiar air conditioning of the fifth floor. Instant nostalgia. The clothes on my back dated me back to the time I was admitted to the hospital. I took off my jacket and removed my tie. Should I go back to my room and start again? I was suffering from a hemorrhage of confidence. In a moment, I might panic and run. I was caught off base, abandoned to the world of melting asphalt. Then the noise popped my ears. University Avenue assaulted my remaining senses, and I was almost hit by the first taxi that came by. What was I doing standing in the street? I got back on dry land and waved at another car. It wasn't a taxi, but the driver waved back. The only disaster I escaped was walking into melting chewing gum. That came later. I'd forgotten all about the sound of the wind whistling down this canyon of high-rise hospitals and head offices. When a cab screeched to a stop, probably saving me from my choice of orthopaedic departments, I jumped into the back seat.

It must have been on my way down to the street that I'd changed my mind about where I wanted to go. My unreasoned fear of the precincts of higher learning led me to soften the blow with a short preliminary detour.

"Do you know Barberian's Steak House?" I asked the driver.

"Who doesn't?" he replied. And off we went to Elm Street. Was that east of the hospital or west? Funny, I could keep track of north and south, but east and west were harder. Was the concept of north hard-wired in my brain? Was east more abstract than south? West more complicated than north?

I had forgotten about riding in a back seat. The weight of my body responded to every turn and stop the taxi made. So, all the way to Elm Street, I felt like a ping-pong ball being bounced about on a bumpy sea. The streets were a mixture of the strange and the familiar. I give myself no marks for knowing the streets of Toronto, but it seemed that the city looked stranger than the last time I was here. And people changed size so quickly: at one moment they were small figures standing on a corner curb, the next they were large faces passing the side of the taxi as it rounded the corner. It made me dizzy.

I remembered, as we pulled up in front, the classic façade of the restaurant: colonial details in black and white. Inside, the bartender was shaking a cocktail vigorously while talking to a busboy. This was the slack time before the lunch-hour rush.

"It doesn't matter whether you use an expensive piece of equipment or an old beat-up oven; it still takes exactly the same time to bake a potato. When Harry started this place, he couldn't afford fancy, so for the first year we used an old household oven. It did great potatoes, and the fancy equipment, when it came, didn't save one minute." The speaker had seen me by now and looked in my direction. "Yes?"

"I'm scouting locations for a film company. Could I look through the restaurant to the back door?" I handed over one of my old dog-eared cards.

"What's the movie?" the bartender asked.

"What's the producing company?" the busboy wanted to know. I saw right away that I'd have to watch him.

"Cinema Arts," I said. "New York company," I added, in case he was going to reach for the local Yellow Pages.

"They made *Return to Paddington Station* last year. With Sarah Coalfax." The bartender frowned.

"Show Mr Cooperman through, Stavro."

Stavro shrugged and led me through two or three rooms, each with a couple of early diners leaning over the white tablecloths at one another: business and pleasure mingling. The walls were hung with oil paintings and engravings with a broadly historical theme. A ledge running along the walls a few feet below the ceiling was devoted to three-dimensional curios: miners' lamps, candlesticks, candle moulds, flint lighters, and all sorts of early home-lighting equipment. It made an impressive frieze. The last dining room led to a preparation area, and that in turn to the kitchen itself with a scullery beyond. Here was a door leading, I guessed, to the parking lot behind.

A dishwasher looked me over. "It's open," he said in heavily accented English. I peered through the door, which opened easily. I tried to remember how to say thank you in Greek, but the word wasn't where I'd left it. The dishwasher seemed to be studying me for a portrait.

"Do you remember an ancient, beat-up Oldsmobile parked out there in early April? It was one the cops were asking questions about."

He threw his head back and clicked his tongue. "I missed all that stuff, like the time the Stones were out front or the time the boss turned up with Harrison Ford. I missed Liz Taylor too. Spiros told me about the car."

"Could you get Spiros to call me?" I found a ten-dollar bill in my pocket and handed it to the dishwasher. While I was laboriously writing out my phone number, making sure I hadn't substituted threes for sixes or other tricks my new mind conjured up, he said that it might take a day or two, because Spiros was off for a couple of days. I told him that it didn't matter, just so long as the message got through.

"Did the cops talk to Spiros?" I asked, watching him run another crowded tray into the machine.

He preceded his answer with a toss of his head and the click again. "He was off that week too. Cut himself on a broken glass. Twenty-six stitches!"

I added another five dollars for pain and suffering, even though it was going to the wrong person. I nodded my goodbyes and turned to the back door.

The lot was small, with a narrow lane between the restaurant and its neighbour leading to Elm Street. A Rolls-Royce was parked behind, along with several other late-model cars and vintage collectors' items. I didn't see my 1986 blue Oldsmobile. I'd have recognized its rusted fenders and skirting anywhere.

I thought of quizzing the help, but my questions would be no better than those the police had asked. And they had asked them when the event was fresh. Remembering my fib to the bartender out at the front of the restaurant, I decided not to prolong my visit.

I walked back through the dining rooms to the front door.

The bartender, now polishing glasses, grabbed me by the upper arm.

"Hey!" I called without thinking.

"When do the cameras roll?" He released me.

"That won't be for months. Besides, that's not my end. I just tell them what I saw. They do all the brain-work. You'll hear from them with lots of warning."

"So I shouldn't hold my breath? Right?"

"You got it." And I got out of there, leaving the bartender with visions of a dazzling film career dancing before his eyes.

NINETEEN

WITHOUT TAKING TIME to catch my breath, I walked to Yonge Street, where I flagged down a second taxi.

"Take me to St Gabriel's Hall in the University of Toronto. It's on St George Street."

"I know it," the driver said, adjusting his mirror to see me better. I grinned back at him. The streets went by in a dizzy whirlwind of strange as well as familiar corners.

"Here you are," the driver announced, just as I had settled down to watching the scenery roll by. I gave him some money from my wallet, a bill of too large a denomination for the driver to change easily. He grumbled under his breath as he stirred himself to find his cache of small bills. "Thanks," he said with naked sarcasm.

St Gabriel's Hall was an old Toronto brownstone, the kind that used to dominate the street on the east side. Nowadays these antiques were getting scarce. I walked along the sidewalk, found the big glass-windowed front door open, and went in.

It was like a stage set. Halls led off in two directions, a fine Victorian staircase rose around and above me, suggesting other destinations. Arrived and ready to quiz somebody, I found the place seemingly deserted. A man tuning a piano in the hallway looked as new to the building as I felt. I peered into a small pantry alcove. Nobody. Then, facing the street, I saw some bobbing heads through a glass door.

I was peering through the glass when a voice behind me demanded: "Are y'looking for somebody, or are y'simply prospecting for a cup of coffee?" The voice was almost that of Sean Connery, the first and best James Bond. In a more compact edition, he resembled him, too, but in his more recent, mellower years.

"I'm … I'm looking for Professor Bett. My name's Cooperman."

"I'm looking for him as well! This is where he'll be, if he's on the campus today. Come in. I'm Angus Kelvin. Call me Angus." He led me into a large, comfortable, old-fashioned sitting room, furnished with leather institutional furniture older than the combined ages of the three men and one woman sitting there. Well, almost. An ancient fern gasped for air by the windows. A mantelpiece clock recorded the presentation of itself to the college but not the time. I was pressed into a seat facing St George Street and three members of the group. Through the closed door, the single notes of the piano could be heard, as one by one the piano-tuner adjusted their pitch. My Scottish friend brought me a cup of coffee and settled himself in the big comfortable chair next to mine. The others seemed to be ignoring the fact that an outsider had penetrated this *sanctum sanctorum.*

"Are you Professor Gladstone?" a man with a neat grey beard asked me.

"No, my name's Cooperman. I'm looking for Professor Bett," I said in an unnaturally squeaky voice.

"It's true: Morgan Bett's often here for coffee." This from a tall, lean man who was looking me over. "Have a biscuit. They bring us these biscuits every Friday and we are expected to eat them. I wouldn't care to speculate on what happens from Saturdays on." He said this with a straight face in a voice that spoke of the southern half of this continent. As a group, they sat on ceremony: there were no introductions, no pack drill. It was like joining a group that had been sitting since the beginning of time. They had no concern for exits and entrances. I reached for a cookie and managed not to spill my coffee.

Plink, plink, went the piano.

"I was looking most particularly for a man I've corresponded with for many years. I think he said he was coming today."

"Name of Gladstone?" asked the tall American with a half-suppressed twinkle, twisting his legs around one another.

"Why yes! Do you know him?"

The remaining man leaned over to me. "Are you the new writer-in-residence?"

"No, I'm not an academic of any kind."

"He's come looking for Morgan Bett."

"Are you one of Angus's acolytes? He doesn't usually bring his fans to coffee."

Plink, plink, went the piano, now moving up into the treble clef.

"Bill, you always pounce on people!" This from a retired professor with an old school tie.

"I didn't pounce! I didn't jump or take advantage. I put it to him in the time-honoured manner. When I pounce, you'll know it."

"It looked like a pounce from here," muttered the grey-haired professor with the tie.

"Well, these things have to be taken up in the right perspective. One man's pounce is another man's spirited sally."

"Morgan often plays chess with Angus," the silver-haired woman whispered to me. From that moment, I began to relax. The conversation sailed around the room, quickly and with spirit.

Plink, plink, plink, went the piano.

"That piano-tuner sounds like he's deconstructing *Liebestraum.*"

"Aye. Why doesn't he go *away?*"

"This never happened in the old tower room."

"Somebody pinched the clock there."

Again the piano sounded. This time with some finality. I sat it out, enjoying their banter. After consuming two cups of coffee and two biscuits, my right to sit among them was still unchallenged. Nobody made me feel odd man out, and two of them smiled at me when they left. It was the nature of the gathering, a bit like a theatre's green room: people were always coming and going. Even Professor Gladstone arrived, much to the delight of his pen pal.

When I asked Angus, the man with Bond's voice, about Dr Bett, he conferred with the man next to him, then reported that my friend was not going to appear this morning.

"Dentist!" he said with a shudder. "I hope you'll come along next week. Aye, he'll be here next Friday. Come see us again."

TWENTY

"WELL!" SHE BEGAN. "You're back! Next time you go off without leave, you might at least take me along. You're not the only one who's tired of these dull walls." Her attempt to look like an outraged fishwife, even with her hands on her hips, was a flop.

"Sorry."

"You've had visitors and I didn't know what to tell them. Dr Collins wanted to see you. I almost told him that you had gone walkabout. But instead I just said that you were getting some exercise."

"Sorry," I repeated.

"All very well for you to—" she began, but she didn't pursue it.

"Who were my other visitors?"

"Oh, those two desperate characters masquerading as police officers in plain clothes. Plain? I ask you. If they thought they could fool anyone in those outfits, they've got another think coming. Pals of yours, I imagine?"

"Sometimes. I don't suppose they said what they wanted?"

"No. They took their secrets with them into the elevator. One of them took a chocolate bar from your box of treats. He seemed to be in charge."

"Anyone else?"

"You have great expectations for a little fellow! No, the line of visitors ended with the servers and protectors."

"I don't know who I was expecting. I have an unquenched desire to see ... I don't know what."

"There's something I can give you for that. There's a pill for everything."

I was surprised she let me off so lightly. I had assumed that I'd be coming back to a royal fuss. This wasn't even a slap on the wrist.

As soon as the nurse left the room, I gave myself up to a deep sleep. I wasn't used to the world *out there*. It was foreign and dangerous, subject to frivolous changes in temperature and humidity. The people *out there* moved guardedly, while gusts of hot air blew scraps of newspapers along the sidewalks, out into the street and up into the air, where they rose like ballet dancers taking flight. Inside the hospital, the weather was under strict control, air-conditioned, unexcitable, dependable, unreal. I was going to have to adjust to reality in easy stages. The sound of the wind blowing down University Avenue, remembered from my excursion, carried me off to sleep under the warm covers. Sleep, the old whore, had cornered me again.

There are all kinds of sleep—refreshing all-nighters, fender-bending nightmares, catnaps, and deep oblivion—but for a sleep that gathers you up, seduces you, and turns off your lights there is nothing quite like hospital sleep. Sleep, the seductress of my waking hours, watched me closely, knew my weaknesses, held out lurid promises. When I was in the middle of dinner or talking to a visitor, she began gathering me into her warm embrace. I didn't usually try to fight it: there's not much competition in a place like Rose of Sharon. Again, I surrendered to her touch, and again, it was good.

Then there were voices, far away, against an echoing background. I can't reproduce the words, not the exact words, one never can in a dream, but there were two voices talking about drugs and their cost. One voice, an English-accented voice, was telling the other not to be daft, that she shouldn't play at knowing what she was doing without measuring the cost. "Ecstasy," she said. "Have you lost your tiny mind?" The other voice was younger, guarding her ignorance with bluster.

"What's the harm?" Where had I heard such talk? Were they nurses talking near my bed? Right now, as I slept? Or were they seeds from my memory, dropped like acorns from my resting brain? Was it a fragment of another time and place? I didn't know, but I awoke with the idea of drugs in my head. And it wouldn't go away.

When I got up, mid-afternoon had arrived. There was a small crowd in the dining room, sitting in front of the TV, a collection of wheelchairs, bumper to bumper, watching

a quiz show. The hostess of the program wore her hair in
two bright blond braids with bows of blue ribbon. She
reminded me of somebody. It was one of those vague
reminders of my former self that kept elbowing my
memory. Maybe I'd get used to it. Of course, now I had
my memory in a book. There should be no confusion.

I got a cup of juice and joined the few of us not
addicted to TV. I talked to the former diplomat for a
quarter of an hour. As usual, I couldn't remember his
name without a covert reference to my Memory Book.
With him was a wizened ghost of a man in a wheelchair,
wearing an ill-fitting, faded hospital gown. He looked
both bright and ill at ease. He was introduced to me, but
his name went where all good names went these days.
He was a newcomer, wheeling himself out of his room
for an early exploration of the corridor, like a kid testing
the overnight ice on the pond. The diplomat had been
talking about the brisk world trade in Canadian passports.
He said that our nationality was now the favoured one
for any fugitive in need of a fresh identity. The old man
and I listened, enjoying an inside peek at international
affairs. He was drinking a cup of cold coffee. I think he
preferred it that way. The diplomat had juice. We sat
together watching traffic roll down University Avenue.
A conversation started. I don't remember where it began,
but like a lot of conversations it drifted from politics to
religion, and from religion to education. The man with
the grey face told a story about his granddaughter
getting an award at an Eastern university. We offered

congratulations and basked in the diluted glory for half a minute.

"What about campus crime? For instance, drugs." I asked him out of the blue. I didn't know my question until I heard myself ask it. Didn't I have a dream about dope of some kind? I retained a vague clot of a memory.

"Drugs?" the diplomat asked, looking at his companion. "Look at the beautiful day out there. Why do you want to talk about drugs?"

"I know some people, a family. Drugs are pulling the family apart."

"You should be asking my friend, Wilf, about drugs. Wilf Carton, Ben Cooperman. Wilf just got here from Toronto General. Wilf's a retired law professor, Benny. Wilf, watch out, Ben's a private eye."

"Private investigator," I corrected to keep the record straight.

The old man's eyes twinkled as he licked his lips. The paper-thin skin of his head was transparent. His right arm hung limply over the arm of his wheelchair.

"Why is the university a good place to have an illegal drug business?" I asked.

While we watched him, Wilf thought for a minute, his eyes on the traffic down below. "I'll tell you," he said. "As you know, the major trade in drugs is done in the great American cities: New York, Los Angeles, Chicago. Smaller, but still significant, is the steady traffic up here, but the big money is down in the States." So far he hadn't added to my knowledge, but I wasn't going to blast him for that yet. He had stated his theme. Now he was going to enlarge on it. "The police do a lot of under-cover work, looking for illicit dealers. In some cities, they have even become dealers themselves, I'm sorry to say. But, with a little intelligence, the dealers manage to stonewall most legitimate undercover operatives." He took a breath and looked like he was about to tell me more when he said, "Where is this friend of yours? Toronto? York?"

"Simcoe College, University of Toronto."

His eyes widened.

"You *know* that place?"

"If I did once, I don't any more." For a minute the conversation was sidetracked to the peculiarities of my hospitalization. Then we returned to the main theme.

"The suspicion is that the labs at Simcoe Collge are being used to manufacture drugs. You'd be looking for a common street drug that can be made in a lab. Doesn't need fancy equipment. But you've got to be careful or you'll be walking around with a drug-induced case of Parkinson's. Whoever's behind the operation at Simcoe has buffaloed the best efforts of the campus police."

I nodded, a buzz beginning in my head. "Have they had any luck?"

"From what I hear, they catch the small operators, but can't get close to the people who are manufacturing the narcotics."

"It shouldn't be hard to locate a lab that's being used to make dope. If you need a lab, don't you have to requisition it? Don't names appear on forms? Isn't anybody keeping records?"

"Ask the police. Now, tell me what you know. First of all, what are we talking about? Heroin? Cocaine? You won't find them in a campus lab except under controlled conditions. Crack? LSD? Ecstasy?"

"Ecstasy. Let's go with Ecstasy."

"Good bet. There, the traders, the young students being picked up, are not informing on the manufacturers, who keep well out of sight."

"So, it's a major problem?"

"The manufacturers will get picked up one of these days and there will be a hiatus."

"Just a pause? Not an end to the trade?"

"Mr Cooperman, I'm too old to be an optimist. It's human nature you're dealing with, a notoriously unstable substance. Young people have been rebelling against the forbidden since Adam was a farmer. What are you going to do?" Wilf Carton went on looking out the window and then turned to look at me again. "If I live to be two hundred, I'll never understand the back streets of human nature, Mr Cooperman. In the contest between Wordsworth and Robespierre, the Frenchman wins every time."

We continued to look out of the window. I couldn't explain this sudden fascination with the tiny cars and trucks down below. Maybe it was because their life went on without any awareness that we were watching. It might have been the fact that we knew something that they would learn later on. Whatever it was, the sight of moving traffic held us like a scene of life on another planet. The cars, the slow-moving figures, all looked foreign, irrelevant to our lives. After five minutes, the picture grew depressing.

I went back to my bed, intrigued by the conversation I'd just had. At the edge of my consciousness was the image of that television blonde with the two braids buttressing her invisible ears. Like a puppy worrying a new pair of socks, my mind kept coming back to it. Where was the key to unlock that fugitive fragment?

I didn't feel as tired as I had earlier, but I didn't have energy for challenge. For a minute or two, I fought the good fight, but in the end my moth-eaten character gave way. I let myself feel the pillow under my head and closed my eyes.

It was moving on toward late afternoon when I woke up. I played a hand or two of gin rummy with my room-mate, Jerry, just to be friendly, and he took me for fifty cents. I never play cards if I can help it, but Dagmar had phoned to say that she couldn't visit Jerry today. He was a decent fellow and that overrode my dislike of card-playing.

The less said about dinner, the better. Somebody told me that the closer you get to being discharged, the worse the food tastes. I can believe that.

"Mr Cooperman?" It was a complete stranger staring down at me as I was courting a post-prandial nap before seriously going to sleep. My visitor was an Indian from India. A few of the specialists I'd seen walking through the corridors were Indian. I wondered whether my pulse had developed irregularities I hadn't been told about.

"That's right. Who are you?"

"My name is Abul Moussuf. I'm a friend of Steve Mapesbury. Over at the university. We talked together, you and I, many, many days ago." He was losing steam, seeing no signs of recognition from my bewildered face. His was the chubby, dimpled face of a boy, promoted to the summit of his six-foot frame. "Remember, we talked about Steve in my lab a few months ago. You came to see me."

"You're Boolie, right?"

His face opened up and the sun came out. "That's what my friends call me, yes." He smiled at this break in the clouds. "You remember now, yes?"

"No. I don't remember. That's why I'm here."

He went on to explain how he tracked me down. Not hard for a trained scientist. "But I am *so sorry* for your trouble. It was a dreadful thing to have happened. I didn't know."

"But perhaps not quite as dreadful as what has happened to your friend. When did you last see Steve Mapesbury?"

"Not since your Easter, Mr Cooperman."

"Call me Benny."

"Benny. Yes, and, please, call me Boolie. Everybody calls me Boolie."

"You're from Kashmir."

"Yes, but I have been living abroad for so many years now that I can hardly remember it sometimes. And at other times it seems so real, I feel I could reach out and touch a familiar tree or stone. It's very beautiful: the

mountains, the rivers, the Vale of Kashmir, the tempo of
life. It's good for the heart, I think."

"Where is your friend?"

"I do not know. We have mislaid ourselves."

"Was Steve mixed up in the drug business going on
over there?"

"I would not care to say."

"Look, Boolie, I'm not a policeman. I'm just looking
for information. I want to find him before somebody tries
to kill him. Hell! He may be dead already for all I know."

Boolie was watching me, trying to decide whether or
not to trust me. At least that was my guess. He had the
sort of face that can hide nothing.

"I worked closely with Steve," he finally said, "when
I first joined the department. We were good friends,
shared digs and an office. But for the past year I've been
busy on other things, loaded with work. Whenever I saw
Steve, I thought, He doesn't look well. Something's not
right. But I didn't get a chance to follow up on my good
intentions. Damn it all to hell! You see, my vibes are from
Kashmir and from England. I don't know where the line is
drawn that lets one ask questions of a once-good friend
who is being evasive. He's a good man, but he's been hard-
pressed. The life of a scientist isn't easy, Mr Cooperman,
and there are temptations."

"Did Steve give in to those temptations, Boolie?"

"I wish I knew. One of his daughters was sick in the
winter. Something expensive."

"Wasn't he covered by insurance?"

"Nowadays there is coverage and *coverage*. There are always expenses with illness, and the health-care blanket that is supposed to cover one is getting smaller year by year."

"Do you think he compromised his principles?"

"I know he put his savings into a down payment. That's not a compromise. I could always tell when mortgage payments became due. He never had pocket money. Not for a long time, and then suddenly he did. He paid me back what he owed me. I hoped that he'd got lucky somehow. I didn't even guess. Then he started looking terrible, like a character in Shakespeare gone off the rails. I should have tried to help him. I should have tried harder." Boolie's face looked as though it was going to melt. He was crying.

I sat up in bed and threw my feet to the floor.

"But, Boolie, you lent him money. You were a big help to him."

"That's very kind of you to say, but, no, I could have done more. It was an omission on my part, a serious omission."

It took me a few minutes to calm Boolie down. He sat on my bed, while I threw the rest of my clothes on. My roommate poked his head in the door and seeing Boolie's tears, wheeled himself to a neutral corner. I passed Boolie the box of tissue that stood handy.

"Boolie, I'm trying to draw up a cast of characters surrounding Steve. Who were his friends and who were his enemies?"

"As far as I know, Mr Cooperman—"

"Call me Benny, please."

"As far as I know, he was being hounded by the police. They were breathing down Steve's shirt collar."

"How did they know what Steve was up to?"

Boolie shrugged.

I thought a moment: "Who else is after Steve?"

"There's a man, part of a supervisory group that has been trying to create a uniformity in the teaching of science subjects. At first, it was to set high standards of professionalism, but it became more of a second set of campus police. He gave students from Southeast Asia a hard time, and set the RCMP on a grad student from Iraq. He hated the way Steve was friendly with his students, had coffee with them on campus, and went with them to a pub after classes. Steve was a popular teacher, and there were those who resented his easygoing manner with his students."

"Who was this vigilante?"

"Yes, that is the right name for him and his like. They despise the very best that a teacher can give. If Dr Samson wasn't so well liked and well respected, they would have even tried to topple *him*. They distrust anybody who makes learning fun. They stopped one teacher from taking a class outside."

"Who are these people?"

"The worst of the lot is Nesbitt. George W. Nesbitt. He singled out Steve and gave him a hard time, starting long before his decline."

"Okay. Now, besides you, who are his allies and friends?"

"For the last few years at least, his mentor has been Parker Samson. He's the head of the biochemistry department."

"Steve's wife mentioned him. I tried to get him, but he's a busy man."

"Parker's a lot like Steve. They are older and younger versions of one another. Parker helped Steve get this appointment at the university. He was on the board that interviewed Steve and a few other candidates. Like Steve, he's down-to-earth. Gets along with the undergrads."

"Does he know Steve's family?"

"I don't think so. I never saw him at their house. And I used to be there quite a lot. I know he's worried about Steve's disappearance. He has talked to me about it."

"Boolie, may I ask you something?"

"But of course!"

"Where did Simcoe College come from in the first place?"

"Simcoe College was founded by three prospectors who made their fortunes in the hard-rock mining country in northern Ontario. All of them came from towns and farms near Lake Simcoe, in what people tell me they call Cottage Country. One unique thing about Simcoe College is that it has no church affiliation. Some of the older colleges were set up by one church or another: St Mike's by the Catholics, Knox by the Presbyterians, and so on. Simcoe has as little to do with the overall university government as it can. And the university people enjoy this arm's-length connection. You understand?"

We talked for another ten minutes or so. Then I remembered that coffee could be found around the corner behind the nursing station. I'd found it there on one of my exploratory rambles. Boolie followed me and made himself comfortable in a chair far too small to contain him. We drank two cups of coffee, sitting at the big table by the windows. I enjoyed his company until I was found by one of my nurses, who dragged me off for a urine sample.

TWENTY-ONE

MY LONG TALK WITH BOOLIE MOUSSUF had put the skin of reality over the people I had been talking to over the telephone. Steve Mapesbury was as elusive as ever, but at least now he had weight and dimensions. And that, as the old history books used to say, was a Good Thing.

The best place to begin the account of what happened next is probably with an early morning phone call I got from Professor Parker Samson. It came right after my rejection of hot cereal. The nurses tried to persuade me, but I stuck to my guns; I wasn't going to throw away a lifetime's worth of abhorrence just because I had lost my memory. Somehow, all my likes and dislikes—in people as well as in food—had escaped intact after my injury. I wasn't even tempted.

"Mr Cooperman? Glad I've finally got through to you there. How *are* you getting on?" Professor Parker Samson identified himself and told me that he had a few minutes before an appointment to help me in my inquiries. I thanked him and tried to remember the questions I'd been asking everybody.

"When did you see Dr Mapesbury last?"

"Oh, that would have been several months ago. We grabbed a bite of lunch one day at the Faculty Club."

"Was he worried about anything at that time?"

"The usual things with Steve: family, money, mortgage, that sort of thing, getting a front tooth fixed. He was worried about missing his classes. But I have some slack in my budget; I was able to patch his absence with a couple of clever Ph.D. candidates."

"Was he at all worried about the police?"

"Oh, you know about that. Yes, he thought that the police were gunning for him."

"And was he right? Drugs are serious. Wouldn't you cut them some slack if they're trying to run down drug pushers?"

"I don't give a good goddamn whether a student smokes a joint now and again. It's all part of growing up. Part of the university experience. I know I did it. I don't care who knows it. I didn't turn to a life of crime and I didn't flunk my courses. If you ask me, and you *are* asking, I think that the experience made me a more rounded person in the end. You see what I mean? The people who are overzealous in cracking down on drugs this week will be asking for loyalty oaths next week. They're the next thought police."

"Are you suggesting that there's something more sinister than drugs?"

"Damned right! There's a dark force, especially around my college, that makes me think of Torquemada and Robespierre. Both the professionals and the amateurs are changing the very nature of academic freedom. They don't give a damn about the spirit of inquiry. Sorry," he said after a pause, "I didn't mean to bend your ear with one of my sermons about academic freedom."

"When you mention the unofficial campus police, who do you mean?"

"They must have been in their heyday during the McCarthy era. No, they aren't old enough. They're all for having all the students and professors sign loyalty oaths. Another leftover from the McCarthy era! Anybody objects, out he goes! Any little international scare brings them out of the woodwork. There are, as I said, a bunch of them. But the ringleader is George Nesbitt. Remember that name, Mr Cooperman! He will put the kibosh on the spirit of toleration and generosity on this campus. His colleagues can't understand who let him in. If anybody could ever induce me to stick pins in a voodoo doll, that man could. God save our civil liberties!"

"Amen, to that! Tell me, Professor Samson—"

"Call me Gauche. That's what my friends call me."

"Good, Gauche. And I'm Ben."

"Sure, Ben."

"What exactly has this fellow been up to with reference to your friend, Steve Mapesbury? Is he trying to get him disbarred, defrocked, or whatever the academic equivalent is?"

"He and his friends have filed a number of reports. I've seen them myself. That goes with my job, Ben. There aren't many on the committee who'd give much time to this sort of back-stairs gossip, but Steve's file is getting bulky. One day we are going to be asked to provide a sacrificial lamb to satisfy some need or other—budget cuts, overstaffing, tightening our belts—and it will be hard not to throw Steve's name into the hat."

"But he's not a rabble-rouser. And since when is it a crime to be a popular teacher?"

"I hear you, Ben! But to be frank and crude at the same time, the boy hasn't watched his back. He takes some classes outside. He skips meetings. He called Professor Nesbitt 'an exhausted fascist relic' at a staff meeting. He is death on people, like Nesbitt, who do no teaching, see no students. He hates so-called scholars who neither publish nor teach. In short, he's not a team player. He was very nearly let go last year, but he'd published a paper in an important learned journal. He's got all the good intentions in the world. Heart of gold. Wants to buy the moon for his little girl's birthday. I'd trust that boy with my life, my bank account, and my wife."

"What about *his* wife? Was he a family man by day and a Lothario by night? I've heard that a student was involved with him."

"It still takes two to tango, Ben. Having young, attractive undergraduates lose their heads over one is one of the hazards of the profession. There may have been some of that in the young student who came to see me, but I think it was mostly concern for Steven's recent attitude. It was getting so that nobody could talk to him. We all tried to bring him down to earth, tried to get him to save some of his energy and scorn for next year. She was worried about him, that's all."

"I see." I was beginning to feel as though I was at a political rally. "You said you met the girl who was looking for Steve?"

"She came to my office. Sweet little thing. What business she had with Steve I don't even want to imagine. Whatever it was, she had it bad. It was all I could do to get her out of my office. And she took a new linen hand-kerchief of mine with her!"

"Have you been talking to Steve's family?"

"I give Laura a call once in a while. Not this week, I admit. But I will. Somebody's got to look out for those girls."

"Gauche, it has just struck me that talking to me must fill you with a feeling of, what is it called? Déjà vu? I mean, didn't I ask you the same questions the first time we met?"

"Some of them, Ben. Some of them. But I don't mind a little repetition in a good cause."

"Thank you for calling me, Dr—I mean, Gauche. You've been a big help."

"Only too glad. And you! You take care of yourself. When are they going to let you return to Grantham?"

"That's the question that I keep asking and they keep dodging."

"Well, good luck! If I get around your way, I might drop in."

"I can't ever get enough visitors. Thanks. Fifth floor."

"I'll find you."

The phone rang again as soon as I hung it up. Never had I been this popular. It was Anna.

"Well, you're in demand all of a sudden!"

"Have you been trying long?"

"I did get the word on your George W. Nesbitt."

"Should I leave town?"

"The people I've talked to say that he is—on certain subjects only—an embarrassment to the college. But he's a donkey for work and he doesn't seem to hear the sniggers around him or see the winks and grins. He's the sort of person who does all of the work that nobody likes to do. He makes himself indispensable and has created a job for life. Nobody respects him or really likes him, but when they talk of getting rid of him, the people who would have to shoulder his workload begin to shuffle their papers and look straight down at the table. People give him slack because he's had a rough go of it in his private life. He lost his wife to lung cancer, and his daughter's been in and out of more schools than lined paper. She's seen a lot of trouble."

"I think I've met her in another life. What else did you get?"

"Wherever I went, I kept hearing about Professor Samson."

"What about him?"

"He's a good administrator, an inspiring teacher, and he has a way with the undergraduates. He talks their language."

"I just got a sample. He phoned me."

"He's been a popular member of this university since his football days. Gauche Samson once scored the winning touchdown with three seconds left in the game. They carried him along Bloor Street all the way to the King Cole Room in the Park Plaza, where the celebration went on until closing time and after."

"Sounds like a first-person account. Were you there?"

"A young woman, even one technically under age, finds that there are good reasons to take her studies of life out into the streets!"

"Across the nation!"

"Around the world!"

"You coming in to see me?"

"When I get back in town. I promise."

TWENTY-TWO

TWO INTERNS CAME AROUND to thump me after breakfast the next day. One was humorous and thorough, the other watchful and silent. Then their supervisor, a brisk woman, all starch, dropped in to see how they were doing.

"Mr Cooperman and I are old friends, aren't we, Mr Cooperman?"

I didn't doubt her word, but I didn't recognize her. She took a look in my mouth using a tongue depressor. I felt six years old.

"Ah-hah! He is crowded back there. Bet he can't brush his teeth without choking." She gave them hell for not checking the back of my throat. They both took note of this before moving on to Jerry in the other bed. I wondered what a narrow throat had to do with my concussion.

One of our remaining gourmets had graduated. His absence was noted at lunch. I took a bit of unrecognizable meat and looked around the room. In another four weeks or so, these chairs will be filled by new bottoms, people who haven't yet even contemplated a brain injury. The faces in the dining room had already changed to a degree; I could tell at a glance which people were here when I arrived and which had come since I got here. It was eerie thinking that the fifth floor had been waiting all those years. I guess everything can be seen in that light; everything from bread at the bakery to grave plots.

"Mr Cooperman! Mr Cooperman!" It was one of the nurses from behind the front desk. I parked my fork on a plate and walked across the corridor. "You have a call on this line." She handed me a phone over the countertop.

"Hello?"

"Mr Cooper?"

"Cooper*man*."

"Whatever. Alecos Soveranides told me to call you. We work at Barberian's Steak House. You know?"

"I'm with you. And your name is?"

"Spiros Skandalakos. I'm dishwasher at Barberian's."

"I know it well. What can you tell me about the people coming out of that battered Oldsmobile and into the restaurant? The day the cops are worried about."

"I thought the police were going to call me."

"They still might. What did you see?"

"A man and a girl. He was older, putting on the pounds, you know, going to fat like a boxer who don't work out any more. He had a black moustache and was wearing sunglasses, so I didn't get a good look at him.

About six feet tall. Maybe six-one. The girl was sort of mousy. Little, with blond hair in fancy curls. Her hair was almost pink."

"Anything else?" I consulted the scribbling in my Memory Book and stalled while trying to translate it.

"Let's see. She had a lot of studs in her ears and one or two in her nose. You know, rhinestones or gold. Good-looking girl, though, in spite of that."

I thought about that for a moment, made some notes I wouldn't be able to read in ten minutes, and went on: "Anything else?"

He kept talking, while I squinted at my book for ideas, but most of what he said simply underlined what I already knew. I thanked Mr Skandalakos and passed the phone back over the counter.

"In future, Mr Cooperman, could you give your own number to your friends? This is a busy line. Okay?"

I promised. I didn't know how he got that number; I'm sure I gave the staff at Barberian's the number of my own phone. I'd been carrying it in my pocket for just such an opportunity.

When I got back to my room, I could see that Dagmar was packing Jerry's clothes into a suitcase.

"We've built a new ramp at home from the drive to the side door. With help, Jerry should have no trouble. The boys saw the work through without a hitch. In two weeks, we'll be back in Switzerland. It's a villa we both know from last summer and the summer before. The mountain air will do us both good."

"A-a-and who will I play c-c-c-cards with?" Jerry said between his teeth.

"Jerry wants to know if your father is going to be travelling in Europe this year."

"My father keeps surprising me. Make sure you leave me your address in Switzerland and I'll pass it on to him."

"Y-y-y-your father has a gift for c-c-c-cards," Jerry said aloud. "He c-c-c-could have been a wealthy man, y-y-you know, Benny."

"I think that there's a family curse working against both of us: whatever we do, it never leads to money. But at least he has his health."

"That's right. You should not forget to say goodbye from us," Dagmar added.

When the time came, I walked to the elevator with them. Jerry managed his wheelchair himself; his wife walked alongside. All of us shook hands awkwardly, then the elevator doors shut us off with the extremely unlikely possibility of our ever meeting again. I tried to imagine my father dealing out cards with Lake Geneva in the background. Something blue, white, and red. Very patriotic: Lake Geneva, Mont Blanc, and Manny Cooperman saying "Deal!"

I made a phone call to my friends in blue, hoping to find Sykes or Boyd holding down an office desk, but they were both away. The best I could do was to leave a message. A moment after I'd hung up, it began ringing again.

"Benny?" On the phone was the unmistakable voice of Stella Seco, the mother of Rose Moss. Our dealings a year ago on a case left me bruised enough for her voice to penetrate any loss of memory.

"Yes, Stella. What can I do for you?"

"Oh, Benny! I just heard where you are! The police told me. That's *terrible*! My department is sending you some fruit and nuts. After the help you gave to this network last year, it's only fair."

"Very thoughtful. Thanks."

"What are the police doing about that poor woman's murder? They won't tell me a thing. It *happened* right behind Rosie's residence."

"Did Rosie know the dead woman?"

"How should I know? She's not here. She's out. Benny, what I called about is this: we don't need your help any longer. Many thanks for what you've already done. *And* your injuries. But that's the end. Will you send me your bill? With receipts, of course."

"Stella, *stop*! You're not my client, *Rose* is. Rose hired me; Rose can fire me. Get her to call me." Stella was trying to paint a picture of a home front with all the fires nicely banked and a fresh apple pie cooling on the counter. But something wasn't right about the picture. Rose hadn't made one attempt to see or talk to me since I got beaned behind her residence. That's a few men short of a *minyan* in my book.

"I frankly don't think you know where she is, Stella. Ask *her* to fire me."

"She just *did*! She's a minor and I'm her mother!"

"She's over twenty-one, Stella. Do you think I didn't talk to her?" I was amazed that I'd said that. Was I starting to remember my conversation with Rose? Was my mind coming back from lunch at last?

"If we need a detective again, we'll get one who's not on life-support. You don't know what that girl's been through."

"Stella, make her some chicken soup. Under that Dior suit beats a mother's heart."

"I have to go. Let me know if you hear anything."

I didn't promise. I didn't have time; she was gone that quickly, leaving me with the dial tone as a ground bass to my recollections of an impossible woman.

Around two in the afternoon, there was a call from Anna. I was having one of my naps, while my new roommate was off seeing a battery of specialists.

"Benny," she said in a breathless voice.

Instead of listening, I asked her, "Anna, is there a drug problem at Simcoe College? I'm thinking of Ecstasy, mostly."

"Depends on your point of view. If you're a consumer, you haven't got a problem. All over the campus, the war against drugs goes on, but at Simcoe the problem stands out. Maybe it's because there are so many labs there. I don't know. Last week a grad student told me that the scene is enlarging. The problem's spreading to other colleges. Why?"

"I'll tell you later. You sound like you've got more important things to say. Spill it."

"Benny, something isn't right!"

"What do you mean?"

"I just got finished talking to Sheila Kerzon here on the campus."

"And?"

"And she says that she hasn't been to see you at the hospital."

"She what?"

"She hasn't come to see you. She didn't know you were in the hospital at all!"

"Does she remember me?"

"She says that she talked to you a long time ago. She wasn't sure of your name."

"Something's out of whack! Anna, could you collect Sheila and get right over here?"

"A girl could try."

"And a full-grown, responsible woman?"

"Three shakes of a dead lamb's tail."

TWENTY-THREE

ON A PIECE OF PAPER I tried to work out where I had been all that time ago after driving my Oldsmobile to Toronto from Grantham. Assuming I came alone by car, I must have parked it somewhere near the university. Here I must have met my contact, Rose Moss. Had she hired me? That was the underlying assumption for everything. *No! I've got more than that.* Stella had tried to pay me off just now. That meant I was on the payroll, working for Rose. If this was true, then it was likely that I'd have met her near or on the campus. Knowing the campus, she probably suggested a good place. Not the steak house. That was too far away, and not quite the place to go for coffee at the start of the job. After coffee, she probably led me around to see a few people who knew Steve and who might be expected to remember where he had gone. I had been attacked and left for dead with poor Flora before the Olds was driven down to Elm Street. I couldn't have been with my client all this time. *Wait! I'm getting things out of order. Or am I?* Soon I'd be mixing Rose up with Flora McAlpine. *Hold on, Flora, I'll get to you next.* All these people without faces. They were getting too abstract for my diminished brain. It didn't used to be like this.

I'd followed that line of reasoning, if that's what it was, as far as it would go. I needed a new beginning. Start with the girl. If the girl who came to see me here wasn't Sheila Kerzon, then there were at least three young women in the case. If it wasn't Sheila who accompanied the heavy through the steak house, then it was Miss X. I had a description of the girl at the restaurant, thanks to Spiros, the dishwasher, and I needed to see Sheila, just to check her out and to pick her brain about who the second woman might have been.

I called the cop shop, hoping to get one or the other of my two former associates.

"Hello?" the voice said. "Sykes."

"Jack, it's Benny."

"Why don't you just roll over and play dead, Benny?"

"What have I done now?"

"A little bird told me that you were over on the campus bothering the professors instead of looking after your dialysis."

"There's *nothing* wrong with my kidneys and I wasn't *bothering* anybody."

"Isn't it amazing how honest citizens will twist a story out of shape just to get you in trouble? I'm sorry I mentioned it."

"About the restaurant, Barberian's on Elm."

"You won't find a better chop anywhere."

"I'll remember that when I've finished exploring the subtle virtues of hospital meals. Did you get only the one description of the couple who dumped my car in the restaurant lot?"

"Please, Benny, give it up. Remember, we're months ahead of you. Do I come over to Grantham and try to catch johns who've run away from their overdue MasterCard accounts? Do I try to muscle in on you when you are standing in the rain under a leaking drainpipe while an unsanctioned love affair is consummated in a run-down motel?"

"Cut it out, Jack! My sense of humour is in the wash. Just give me a couple of straight answers."

"Okay, I was just riding you because you sound so fit. They must be getting ready to discharge you one of these days."

"Well, they haven't told me about it yet. Or if they did, I can't remember. About Barberian's. You can tell me. Remember, you're talking to a sieve. It won't come back to haunt you."

"Yeah, yeah, yeah. The dishwasher's was the only description we got: the male suspect had dark glasses and a moustache and the woman had feathery blond hair in a short cap around her head. That's it."

"Did you find anything in my car?"

"Nothing pertinent to the investigation. We found an ancient pair of swimming trunks and a few remains of once noble corned-beef sandwiches. There was a neatly packaged chopped-egg sandwich, which was still viable. This piece of evidence has disappeared."

"What about the driver's seat?"

"Ah! You finally hit pay dirt! It had been pushed back as far as it could go. The driver of your car was several inches taller than you are. Happy?"

"Delighted. Thanks. I'll get off your back. Oh! By the way. The dishwasher you talked to doesn't remember as much as the one you didn't talk to. Name of Spiros Skandalakos. Shall I spell it? See you."

"Hold on! You're not out of the woods yourself, Benny. Because we've confirmed that Flora McAlpine— Remember Flora? The dead woman in the Dumpster beside you?—Flora came from *your* hometown and that she was at the *same* high school you attended and at the *same time*. You try to remember Flora, Benny. There's a good picture of her in your old school yearbook."

"There are eight hundred other pictures in that yearbook! Give me a break."

"Okay, chalk it up to coincidence. But how do you explain that your name appears in Flora McAlpine's appointment book on the day of her death? So long."

I hung up, still hearing Sykes's voice in my head. The name of the murdered professor had always rung a distant bell, but now there were serious links between me and Flora. What kind of case could the boys weave from that? I wondered.

Suddenly the room was full of my parents. I wasn't expecting them, but the passive side of my new nature moved over to accommodate them.

"Benny, I want you to know that I've talked to the rabbi about your situation," my mother said.

"Just keep it simple. Donations to a worthy charity."

"Not about *that!* You used to be so serious, now you're always joking. A regular comedian."

"Sorry. What did Dr Fischell say, and what about?"

"Dr Fischell? That was three rabbis ago! The new man said that according to our traditions it's no sin not keeping kosher in a place like this. The tradition says: Don't make waves if it causes other people a problem."

"So I can go on eating the food in here without endangering my immortal soul?"

"Still the comedian! But you've got the essentials. Anyway, I brought you some sweets. I was looking for the kind with liquid cherry centres, but I couldn't find them."

"It's just as well. My friend Staff-Sergeant Sykes is putting on weight whenever he comes to visit me. Put them under my bathrobe."

Pa, who hadn't said a word so far, was looking through a gap in the curtains toward my new roommate. He had the look of someone who desperately needed a fix: gin rummy, poker, anything.

TWENTY-FOUR

"MR COOPERMAN?"

"Uh-huh."

"Ben Cooperman?"

"As close as I can tell. Who wants him?"

"This is Dr Bett. Morgan Bett. You've been trying to reach me? Angus Kelvin told me."

"Oh *yes,* Professor. You're a friend of Steve Mapesbury's, right?"

"Yes, I am. Have you heard from him?"

"That's what I was going to ask you, professor. I understand that you've been a friend of his for some years?"

"Yes. I have been a friend of the family, you might say. But what's happened to Steve is more than I can imagine. I'm sorry. Wish I could help more."

"Maybe you can. What do you know about Boolie Moussuff?"

"First-rate scientist, good teacher, and a proven friend of Steve's. Salt of the earth."

"What about Parker Samson?"

"He's been a good friend, too. He's watched out for the boy since he first came to Toronto. He helped the boy out, even when he had problems of his own."

"Such as?"

"Well, family trouble. His wife, you know, drinks. And his brother, up in Holstein, well, I don't want to carry tales."

"Forget it. What do you know about Steve's wife and family?"

"Wonderful woman, fine kids. She gives piano lessons, used to be a concert artist in England."

"Sounds like her. Are they still happy together?"

"If anybody is, I suppose they are. There've been tough times, as you may have heard, but I think they are good for each other."

"Professor Bett, thanks for helping out."

"I don't suppose I told you anything new. I'll call again if I hear any news or if I think of something."

"Thanks. *Oh!* Do you know a teacher named Fiona or Flora McAlpine?"

"Why yes, I did, until her lamentably early death."

"What can you tell me about her in relation to Steve Mapesbury?"

"Nothing. I'm surprised to hear they knew one another."

"Was she worried about the spread of drugs from Simcoe College?"

"She talked of nothing else. She was said to be build-ing a case about the traffic in illicit drugs, which she

intended to make known to the Board of Syndics. Her loss
will be difficult to repair, I daresay. Is there anything else?"

I thanked him again and disconnected. I tried to jot
down what I remembered of the conversation in my
book. I had a lot in the book. When I flipped through the
pages, I wondered whether I could ever find something
I needed in that welter of scribbling and attempts at
printing with block letters.

Anna walked in with her hair in a mess and a flush in
her cheeks. I liked her like that. Many women achieve
the impression of beauty in repose. Anna looked fine
that way too, but movement and activity added the *je ne
sais quoi* that delivered the knockout punch. With her
was someone I'd never seen before, a young woman in
her early twenties. She wasn't one of the people I'd met
since coming here to the Rose of Sharon Rehabilitation
Hospital. She was wearing a blue-green sleeveless blouse
of crisp cotton. Her slacks were off-white. The woman
herself was harder to pin down. She looked worried,
impatient, nervous, and shy. Altogether she was a fetch-
ing young woman: pretty, bright, with impressive poise
for her age. She was about the same age as the young
woman who had come to see me a day or two ago who
claimed to be Sheila Kerzon. Coincidence could hardly
account for two Sheila Kerzons walking into my sick
room. There had to be a serious attempt at deception
here someplace.

"It's getting to be a steam bath out there, Benny.
You certainly picked the right time to be surrounded

with air conditioning. This, Benny, is Sheila Kerzon.
Sheila, Benny Cooperman. So much for introductions.
I'll let the two of you talk. I'm going to see if I can scare
up some coffee." She was talking a mile a minute, just at
my level of comprehension and, just as quickly as she had
arrived, was gone again, leaving the two of us to sweat out
the awkward stage together.

"You really *are* who you say you are?"

"Anna checked me out with half a dozen of my
friends. Besides, my driver's licence has my picture on it.
As a picture, it's not great, but you can tell it's me."

She was a taller version of herself than the last edition.
But there was a roundness to her. Puppy fat? Hormones?
I don't know, but it all fitted together nicely, topped off
with blond hair, a round face, and an incipient
Churchillian chin.

"Okay, you're *you:* Sheila Kerzon."

"Always have been." We were sitting across from one
another. She was looking me in the eye for most of her
answers. I believed her story. But then, who am I to judge?
I believed the last story, too.

"Have you ever seen me before?"

"No. Anna told me what happened to you. I'm sorry.
I hope that you keep improving. It sounds like such a
downer not being able to remember things."

"Yeah. But they tell me I'm getting better."

"Rosie talked about you months ago, when Dr
Mapesbury went missing. She said you'd done some work
for her mother."

"Yeah, that's right. So who do you think is trying to pass herself off as you?"

"Could you describe her to me? Otherwise I really haven't a clue."

"She was about your age, maybe a little older. She had the air of someone who had been around a lot. At the same time, she could blush and show her embarrassment. You're taller than she is."

"What about her colouring?"

"She had straight, brown hair, I remember. Yeah, brown with, you know, lighter highlights. She was well dressed enough so I didn't wonder what she was doing here. Know what I mean? She wasn't too tall. Oh, yeah, I think she wore a few studs in her ears and maybe one in her nose. She was wearing a black skirt and was carrying a cardigan. She had long legs and crossed them a lot."

"Men always notice that."

"Do you know who it was?"

"It was our *other* roommate, Heather Nesbitt."

"Nesbitt as in George W. Nesbitt?"

"That's her father. How do you know him?"

"I'll tell you someday. What's Heather like?"

"She's not at Simcoe College to get an education. She's not even trying to find a husband. Maybe, for her, it's just a cool place to hang out."

"Do you like her?"

"After you've been roommates with certain people, I don't think you can ever be friends again. I mean, I like her and all that, but I never could trust her. Not like Rosie.

Rosie's straight, or maybe we're both bent the same way. But Heather is always into things, some of them pretty shady. The bottom line is that I love Rosie and always will. She's great! Heather I wouldn't trust to take the garbage out."

"Does she have a boyfriend?"

"Yeah." She stretched out this word as though she was trying to remember some of the ancient background. "Yeah, but I don't know very much about him. He's older. He's married. And he works at or near the university. I think he's well-to-do. At least, he can afford to give her expensive presents."

Anna returned to the room, armed with coffee in paper cups. I'm not sure how far she had to go to get it.

"Well," she said. "What's the verdict?"

"This is the real Sheila Kerzon. The imposter was Heather Nesbitt, her roommate. And, in a minute, without a net, I'm going to see if I can guess my own name."

TWENTY-FIVE

SOME SECONDS AFTER THE CRACK OF DAWN, my phone started ringing. I cursed the dark for a minute before picking up the instrument to silence it. (There's a lot to be said for cursing the dark, in spite of the optimists out there.)

"Hello?" I tried to say in a pleasant voice, but failed miserably.

"Mr Cooperman? Is that you? This is Abul Moussuf, from the university."

"Boolie! What's happening?"

"We talked about Steve?"

"Yes, Boolie. I remember our conversation." This was only half true. Conversations seemed to disappear into limbo these days. But I remembered the man well enough; his face jumped out of my memory file and I could imagine him at his end of the wire. The burden of Boolie's message was that he and a few of the old professors wanted to visit me and shower me with chocolates and university gossip.

While he was still on the phone, a plan was beginning to form in my pointed head. What about gathering together the people concerned in my current inquiries and bring them to the hospital? It would be easier than my trying to get out of here. It would be like an old-fashioned mystery novel, with the detective pointing the guilty finger on the last page. It was worth a try, I thought, and immediately enlisted Boolie to round up some of the people from the university. From my Memory Book, I read the names and numbers of people he might miss. Before he left the line, he sounded as excited about this conspiracy as I felt.

I was touched that friends of such recent acquisition should have taken any interest in my situation. So moved and honoured was I, in fact, that I called up all of the other people whose numbers were known to me and invited them to a party on the fifth floor at the Rose of Sharon at eight that evening. While I was at it, I called Sykes and his pal, and asked if they might urge everybody involved to attend. I told Sykes what I was up to, after he promised to bring some booze. I didn't check with my nurses. I'm sure they had rules about entertaining suspects without a prescription. If anybody asked, I'd say, "The alexia made me do it." And to hell with critics.

"You're waving a red flag at a bull, Benny. I'll see you around eight this evening and I'll bring a van of well-wishers with me," Sykes said. I could hear the sound of his teeth gnashing as he disconnected.

With company coming at 8:00 p.m., I was hard pressed to know what to do for the mob. I asked my nurse, Rhymes With. She was amazed that I was even thinking of entertaining here on the fifth floor. But having expressed her shock and outrage for the record, she began making plans. She had an accurate notion of what party goods were available on the floor and where others might be found nearby. She wouldn't go along with bringing in a few bottles, but she said that she would underwrite the ginger ale and soda personally. Anna, when she heard, volunteered to get some sandwiches from a university caterer, and I was surprised to hear, as the day began slipping by, that Barberian's Steak House had agreed to send over some fancy Hungarian pastries for dessert. I suspected the untainted fingers of the local homicide squad in this, but I never found out for sure. Maybe it was a bribe to make sure the restaurant was used in the movie they'd heard about somehow. Who knows?

It wasn't hard to put in the time between the moment I'd been fool enough to issue all those invitations and eight o'clock. There were all of the usual hospital routines to get through. I gave both blood and urine. I was thumped on the chest by one doctor and banged on the back by his associate. I was wheeled across the street to see about a sleep test for some night later that week. Even the daily march of the doctors through the corridors, like swallows returning to Capistrano, became a sort of charade, with all the patients encouraged to put up a brave front and minimize complaint.

Dinner was uneventful.

Around five minutes after eight the guests began to arrive. Professor Angus Kelvin and his friends from coffee time unloaded their contributions of food and drink on a table in the centre of a middle-sized reception room off the main corridor, a room for quiet family gatherings. The stranger with Angus, one of the retired professors, I assumed was Morgan Bett, the man who had given me an important piece of the puzzle. My tricky mind tried to remember whether we had ever met or had merely spoken on the telephone. Standing shyly at the door until I pulled him into the room, was A. K. Moussuf. Soon he was beaming at everybody and passing a bottle of bubbly grapefruit juice.

Dr Parker Samson came in looking somewhat surprised, but he joined in talking to colleagues he knew. It was his height that gave him away, even before he came over to shake my hand. He was a big man: not just tall, but solidly made, on the cusp of corpulence. To add to the party, my three therapists from gym, speech, and OT joined the merry throng. I could now remember their subjects even though their names still hovered above my head just beyond the grasp of my memory.

The fancy cakes from Barberian's Steak House were a great hit, along with some sweetmeats that Boolie had brought. "I tried to find something from the subcontinent, but I had to buy these from a little Turkish place."

Toward the back of the room, my friends from the forces of law and order had insinuated themselves. There was an out-of-doors-ish look to them, as though they had been taken from their rural setting and banished to the city's streets. Jim caught my eye and winked.

Gradually, I realized that it was time for me to say something. The number of people facing me made me wish that a stretcher team might come in and carry me off to a place where my lines were written for me and where I had no doubts.

"Thank you for coming," I heard myself say. I tuned in more closely to hear more, but nothing came.

I had reached the end of the prepared portion of my pitch. The silence shouted my cue to action and I jumped into the abyss of the unknown. "It was more than three months ago that Dr Steven Mapesbury disappeared from the university. When I tried to find him, at the urging of his devoted student, Rose Moss, I was waylaid, hit on the head, and left bleeding in a Dumpster almost under the suspended O at Wessex and Spadina. Luckily, I was found and, eventually, brought here to get my wits back or learn to live without them. A professor, a woman named Flora McAlpine, was found in the Dumpster, too. Only she was dead.

"Was Steve Mapesbury kidnapped? If so, it wasn't for ransom. He is a poor professor, not a millionaire, and the kidnappers haven't communicated with his family. What other reason might there be to pull a man out of his everyday life and either kill him or hold him against his will? The kidnapper wants to ensure that Steve doesn't reveal some incriminating information."

"Where is Steve? Why aren't the police looking for

him? That's their job." It was one of the retired professors.

"More to the point," another voice chimed in, "where do you expect this exercise to lead? Do you think you can turn him up with this hackneyed, paperback sort of game? Besides, this sort of deductive reasoning is like moving a dozen beans around on a plate: however you arrange them, they still add up to twelve." This was from someone I didn't know. From the back of the room, Staff-Sergeant Sykes mouthed the name "Nesbitt." I noted Nesbitt's rudeness to the old professor who had spoken just before him. Nesbitt's was not a subtle personality.

"The collecting of facts, Professor Nesbitt, is an orderly, scientific process. When assembled, they sometimes yield new information that wasn't visible before."

Nesbitt screwed himself deeper into his chair, but said nothing.

"Where was I?"

"You were leading us through possible reasons for Steve Mapesbury's disappearance."

"Thank you, Professor Samson. Yes, now what is happening on the campus that Steve is likely to have known about? The selling of essays? Advance copies of examinations? I gather that trade in such items can be brisk. But Steve isn't well connected outside his own department. What else is there?" I paused long enough to run my tongue along my dry lips, then started in again:

"Drug trafficking around Simcoe College has been a problem for some time now. It is serious and threatens to spread to other parts of the university."

"That might be hard to prove," said Nesbitt. "The university has its own watchdogs. We don't need outsiders on our campus."

"I'm not presenting a paper, Professor Nesbitt. I'm drawing pictures in the sand with a pointed stick. So bear with me. For a moment, let's assume that Steve was mixed up in the making of illegal drugs. He had the science background; he had a pressing need for money. His students have mumbled about a subtle disintegration in his preparation of lectures, at processing assignments, and marking papers. He was preoccupied and careless, something he'd never been before. He was being well paid for his part in the drug business. His wife told me there'd been money for jam lately. So what was his worry? I suggest to you that he'd had enough. He wanted out. The fact that about this time he lost an expensive false front tooth suggests to me that his partner in crime didn't appreciate Steve's sudden scruples. They had a fight and Steve got the worst of it. He was now a liability to his boss, the organizer of this illegal trade, and so it was this person who took Steve out.

"When a student, Rose Moss, began asking questions, our criminal would have been wise to get rid of her as well. But her mother got her out of the way instead. I suspect that she's visiting an aunt in Florida until all this blows over.

"We know that someone murdered Flora McAlpine and tried to kill me. He went to my office in Grantham and removed notes from my desk, making it look like a random burglary. So, our heavy deals in damage control. He is dangerous and capable of doing what he thinks is necessary." I needed a drink of water, but there wasn't anything near me.

"Now, drug dealers are not the most savoury of people. They battle for territory and are always knocking one another off. Was Steve a dealer in this sense? I don't think so. Steve was the scientific brains of the outfit. Why would the street pushers kill the source of their supply? The goose that lays the golden eggs.

"So, this was an internal dispute. Steve wanted out, he wanted a bigger share of the profits, he wanted billing? Who knows? Our heavy gets rid of him and then later he gets rid of me and Professor McAlpine." I paused, not just to catch my breath, but to try to remember the thread of my argument. I recalled that mental activity was not my strongest suit any more. I kept seeing the steps ahead and then losing my way. I was also forgetting the names of the people involved. Without my Memory Book with its notes, and lists of names, and even diagrams, I'd have been dead and buried. It gave me the courage to stand there, spouting. I took another breath, but didn't get to the thought I was clinging to before I was interrupted.

"This is all very interesting, Mr Cooperman, but what does it tell us that we didn't know already?"

"Well, it's closed some avenues that we don't have to look down any more, and it has sharpened the focus on what and whom we are looking for. Does that help, Professor Nesbitt?"

Nesbitt grumbled. I wasn't going to turn him into a fan in a hurry.

"What sort of master criminal are you looking for, Mr Cooperman?" This from Staff-Sergeant Sykes, with his back to the window and his mouth half full of cake.

"Well, you told me that from the evidence of the driver's seat in my car, our suspect is a tall man, over six feet in height."

"That's a start," said Boyd.

"True. We also know almost certainly that the man who hit me on the head must have been left-handed. The blow hit me from behind and injured the left side of my head. It would be hard to hit someone that way with the right hand." I turned to show the people where I had been hit.

"Unlike the investigations I've done in the past, where I could get around more and interview the witnesses and suspects myself, I have had to rely on my friends, mostly Dr Anna Abraham, for my information. But I did use the telephone to talk to most of you here this afternoon. I remember talking to Steve Mapesbury's young daughter on the telephone. She was hoping for a call from her father because it was her birthday."

"Very touching, I'm sure, but what does it tell us?" Nesbitt fairly tripped over his heavy sarcasm.

"Actually, it tells us quite a lot. When I was talking to Dr Samson about Steve, he said that he had been worried about getting his daughter something special for this important day. Isn't that right, Dr Samson?"

"Yes."

"It didn't seem to me to be strange at the time, but it has been gnawing away at me. Does the father of two little girls worry about a birthday present months before the event? No doubt a few such daddies exist, but in general? I doubt it. A week before the event, maybe, but months? That seemed like a long time to me. But then, I'm unmarried and without children." Various members of the group in front of me conferred on this point, nodding and shaking their heads.

"Admittedly, this is a weak string. But there are others: his height and his left-handedness. Not enough here to weave a rope."

"Since you have used my name, Mr Cooperman, and since you have made some serious allegations, I think that this has gone far enough. Is there any reason why I cannot leave, Officer?" This from Professor Samson.

"None whatsoever," Sykes said, making a broad gesture with his hands.

"Well, then, I'll take my leave. You may be assured, Mr Cooperman, that my lawyer will be in touch with you."

He gathered himself importantly and stormed out of the room.

TWENTY-SIX

THERE IS NO OTHER WORD FOR IT: Parker Samson's exit was *dramatic*. It was done with panache, with breathtaking effect, and just enough bravado. Those of us remaining in the room were left feeling as though we'd been watered down by a firehose. It was like the TV went dead in the last minute of a cliff-hanger ball game. The shock was perfect, like a musical note held beyond probability. The gesture lacked only one element: durability.

Then the spell was broken. Gauche came back into the room, looking older. Gone was the truculence, the cold sneer, the bearing of spoiled rectitude. He walked slowly and for once seemed completely unaware of his audience. His eyes were on the floor. It was painful to look at him.

Behind him, walking between two uniformed female police officers, came the young woman who had intro-duced herself to me as Sheila Kerzon, Rose Moss's roommate. The wind had gone out of her sails, too. She didn't look at any of us. Her face was marked with defeat. The cops led her to a chair and she sat down automatically, still not focusing on any of us.

After what seemed about a year and a half, George Nesbitt moved away from the people with whom he had been standing.

"Heather? *Heather,* what are you *doing* here?" he said.

The girl looked up for a moment and dropped her head again. She said nothing. Nesbitt looked at her in silence for a moment, then looked at me with eyes demanding me to make sense of this situation.

"What are you trying to pull off here, Cooperman? What are you trying to do to me?"

I tried to think of something to say, but I wasn't thinking fast enough to satisfy Nesbitt. He was halfway across the room with his fists tightly knotted before Boyd stepped in front of him and eased him into a chair in a neutral corner beside Sykes. The fire seemed to go out of him as he was handled by these professionals. In a moment, he was as quiet as a brick wall.

On his way back to where he had been standing, Boyd slipped a piece of paper into my hand. On one side was a cluster of words I couldn't read, ending at a tear through a line of type. The tear told me that the text on this side wasn't what I should be trying to decipher. (Later on, I slowly worked out that the note was an invitation to hear Henry Oughtread, a former patient, speak about his rehabilitation. It was dated three months back.) The real surprises were on the other side in Boyd's messy handwriting. I slowly worked it out and was glad I did.

Once again, the people were looking at me as though I could answer all of their questions at once. Somebody slipped a cool drink into my hand and I started rummaging for the right words. "I'm sorry for that somewhat sensational demonstration. I think we have no more dramatic effects up our collective sleeves. Just to explain about Dr Samson's sudden return, I would suggest that he has more than a routine interest in the young woman who has just joined us. She is Heather Nesbitt, the daughter of George W. Nesbitt, the gentleman over there." I indicated where the girl's father was sitting. He still looked confused and angry, but just managed to remain quiet.

"According to this note," I said, waving it for all to see, "Heather was arrested at Pearson Airport, where she had bought a one-way ticket to New York."

"Damn you! You're making that up!" Nesbitt was on his feet again and in full fury now: red in the face and loud. "Goddamn it, this is my life you're playing with, Cooperman. It's not a clever parlour game." One of the cops, very gently, forced him back into his seat. The force was professional, but not brusque or unfeeling.

"In this note, passed to me a minute ago by Staff-Sergeant Boyd, are all the details. If you want to argue this, he's the man with the facts, Mr Nesbitt."

Instead of moving on to Boyd and arguing things with him, Nesbitt became deflated and sank deeper into his chair.

Judging from the eyes staring at me, a few questions were hanging about in the air. I made a stab at answering them:

"Earlier this week, I think it was this week—you'll have to forgive me on matters of time—Heather came to see me here at the hospital. She came twice, in fact. I missed her the first time; I hadn't yet caught up with my memory. That time she claimed to be my wife. The second time she borrowed the name of a friend, one of her roommates. 'Three little maids from school,' and all so different.

"In early April, I was hired by Rose Moss, the daughter of an old schoolfriend and former client, to find out what had become of one of her professors, Steven Mapesbury. I then drove here from my home in Grantham. I met Rosie on the campus or near it. Shortly after that, I was clobbered and ended up here. Flora McAlpine was less fortunate. How do I know that Heather played a part in what happened to Flora and me? The truth is that I *don't*. Not completely. Toronto police have found, among the belongings she was taking with her to New York, a wig that matches the account given by a dishwasher at Barberian's Steak House as part of his description of the woman who dumped my car behind the restaurant. Her height and colouring match. The wig makes the identification more certain, but not absolute."

Dr Samson tried to cross his legs, but the girth of his thighs would not cooperate. At last, after several tries, he gave it up. His gaze seemed to be drawn to the impassive face of Heather Nesbitt. She looked straight ahead, as if she were alone in an empty room. The two policewomen flanking her kept alert, but didn't seem to be trying to keep up with what was going on in the room. There were still fragments of the refreshments on two or three trays. I snagged a dumpling filled with flavoured rice and wrapped in a vine leaf. It was good enough to snag a second and gobble that, too. When my mouth was empty again, I started talking again.

"Dr Samson has, almost from the beginning, struck me as the perfect suspect in the disappearance of Steve Mapesbury and his student. He is well placed in the scientific community. He knows the missing man. He has a good reputation here at the university, which he would not like to see damaged by the kind of exposure that he may have thought Steve was threatening. There had been arguments: Steve lost a front tooth. An implant. His wife told me that, and that he lied about how it had happened. Samson took Steve from the campus on Good Friday, when the campus was all but deserted. That was the last day Steve's wife saw him.

"A week or so later, Samson reacted strongly when Rose Moss was on the campus with me asking questions. He had to get rid of both of us. Somehow, Rose escaped, probably not even realizing her danger. Rose's mother got her out of the way. Although she didn't admit it, she knew all about my role in this when I talked to her. In our second conversation, she *did* admit it. How Flora McAlpine got mixed up in this, I don't know. There is some evidence that I had questioned her, or was about to, when we both were targeted. Had she played some part in the drug racket? I don't know. I doubt it."

"Excuse me, Mr Cooperman." It was one of the professors. "I know that this is going to be a long and complicated narration, but please make a bigger attempt to keep to the subject. You were talking about Dr Samson and why you think he might be implicated. True, he is tall and would have had to move the driver's seat back in order to drive your car. What else do you have?"

"My main piece of evidence is so subjective I hate to mention it. It's the sort of thing that would never be admitted as evidence in a court of law. I told you—that is, I *think* I told you—that when I was first here at Rose of Sharon, I was plagued with a nightmare. It was about a train wreck."

"Are we sinking to divination now? Is this a seance? What sort of voodoo is this?" Nesbitt was showing signs of revival.

"Sorry. Blame it on my poor head." I tried to find the nub of the tale I was telling, experiencing a moment of total confusion. I couldn't talk. I couldn't think. What the hell was I doing here pretending to be in my right mind? I tried to look at Anna. Anna was always a source of calm. She restored my centre of gravity.

"The dream ... in my dream ... a suitcase flew at me ..." I tried to start again. "I ... I ... I believe that psychiatrists are right when they say that dreams are ways in which the subconscious tries to inform the conscious mind of what it knows."

"This is beginning to sound like a movie from the nineteen fifties, Mr Cooperman: *Three Faces of Eve, The Seventh Veil, Spellbound.*"

"Yes. Do you mean us to take this seriously?"

"Frankly, I don't care what you do with it. All I know is that I'm compelled to tell somebody. It won't take much longer."

"But what was the special meaning of a flying suitcase?"

"Good question, Anna. In this case, the airborne piece of carry-on luggage, which I saw in great detail as it flew through the air with other debris, was one made by the famous American luggage maker, the Samsonite Company. The dream was trying to put the name "Samson" into my head in an important, overriding way."

"So, you have a dream and the possibility of finding a tall, left-handed man, presumably with a driver's licence. Not very much to take with you into a court of law, Mr Cooperman."

"I know it doesn't seem like much, but there's more. We have all seen how he walked out of here: defiant and unpenitent. In less than a minute, he returned, because this young woman, to whom charges may also apply, was being brought into this room."

The people looked away from me to examine the faces of the two suspects. In a way, even as one of his victims, I felt sorry for Samson. Not because I sympathized with what he had done or that I thought there were any exten-uating circumstances that made him a man to be pitied. My sympathy came from the fact that Samson would never see that he had crossed the line, that society was right and he was wrong. He'd go to prison feeling the victim of a short-sighted, backward society, a martyr to these unenlightened times. He was venal, predatory, and scheming, but he was also pushed beyond his limits and in thrall to an overwhelming passion. He was protecting his reputation in the firmament of the academy.

From where I was sitting, Samson looked smaller, as though he'd suddenly lost sixty pounds. His eyes were downcast, directed at the floor. He seemed without hope or even hope of hope.

Then it was all over. Quite suddenly, I was awakened from the unreal dream of playing detective, playing at living in the world outside these walls. At this point, Rhymes With came into the room.

"Sorry," she said. "We need the space for half an hour." There were three doctors and five nurses at her back.

Sykes and Boyd ushered their suspects from the room. They moved like they'd been shackled with heavy chains all the way to the elevator. Holding a handkerchief to his forehead, a perspiring Nesbitt followed close behind. After that, the few remaining sandwiches held little interest for those of us left in the room. Anna and two of the nurses helped me to tidy the room.

That night, nursing a bellyache, I had a long conversation on the phone with Sykes. By the time I'd finished, there was nothing keeping me from my rest that a couple of antacid pills couldn't cure.

TWENTY-SEVEN

I WAS STILL STUCK in the hospital, but Rhymes With let slip that they'd be releasing me soon. How soon? She couldn't exactly say, except that it would be within days, not weeks.

Anna called and suggested we meet for dinner at a restaurant behind the hospital. Sykes and Boyd invited themselves along.

The restaurant was only a short walk from where the last of the fifth floor gourmets were talking *boeuf en daube* and cassoulet to a timorous newcomer.

The restaurant specialized in, as I soon discovered, the hotter sort of Chinese cooking. My guess was that it was developed to ensure that only the hardiest of its regular customers survived.

Anna looked on as a blush coloured my cheeks. She managed not to decorate her pretty face with the food, while delicately using chopsticks to put away her share of spicy beef with orange peels. (I had had to request more conventional cutlery.) The two cops introduced a true meeting of east and west: they skewered their meat with a single chopstick. They dabbed at their faces after most of the damage had been done. They were wearing plain clothes as usual.

Some of the dishes were so spicy they made ordinary cold water taste scalding hot. We were all hungry and in no mood to talk until the bulk of the meal had been reduced to rubble in the middle of the table. Sykes ordered more orange beef, saying we should have ordered two portions to begin with. Boyd picked at a tooth with the corner of a rolled traffic ticket, and I dabbed at my face with a napkin. Except for a ladylike belch, Anna emerged unscathed.

"Benny's eating up a storm, Anna. Don't they feed him in that place?"

I jumped in to defend the hospital: "Hospital food is designed for the rapid circulation of patients. Nobody can stick it long. Right now, I'm enjoying the break. Now, Jack, show some genuine pity on a poor shut-in and tell us the latest news. What's happened to the suspects, Samson and his girlfriend?"

"It'll keep. Enjoy your meal."

"I've enjoyed it! It's now starting the digestive process. You want to wait that out too?"

"Okay. Okay. What do you want to know?"

"The lot." Anna said. I liked the way she used these British expressions. I wonder when she collected them.

"Everything!" I added at the same time.

"Well," Sykes said, looking at his partner's face for an enabling look, confirmation of Boyd's agreement that he was about to spill more than the police normally tell citizens outside a courtroom. His partner's eyes widened, but he was smiling.

"Sure, we might as well. Benny got this case moving again. He deserves to be in at the kill."

Anna caught her breath and my hand under the table.

"Luckily," Boyd added quickly, "it didn't go far enough for a real kill."

"Yeah, everybody came quietly, just as we suggested."

"Hold on!" I said. "What have you been up to? I thought you had them in custody when they left the hospital the other day."

"We couldn't hold them long on what we learned at the hospital. And Samson got the fastest lawyer in town on the case," Sykes said.

"So, they walked?"

"Will you let me finish? Anyway, you should know. It was your suggestion. Do you remember calling me the night of your big hospital soiree?"

"Of course I do!" I lied.

"We put a team to watch Professor Samson. It was expensive: six men, in three shifts. He ended up driving out of the city to a place called Holstein. Ever heard of it?"

There were no responses. Then I remembered that Professor Bett told me something about a village of that name, but I couldn't remember enough of what he had said to add anything.

After a polite pause, Sykes picked up the story. "It's a tiny place; used to be on the main CN line to Owen Sound, but that went for scrap metal years ago. There's a creamery, a blacksmith, and a feed mill. Across from the mill, which is still worked by water, there's a funny-looking house set into the bank of the Beatty Saugeen River." He took a breath. "Steve, the missing professor, was being held inside."

"But you couldn't have followed Samson all the way by car. He would have seen you," I said.

"Hell, we had to drop back after he left the 400. Fellow from Brampton named Red Cavers picked him up from the air. He has a couple of copters he uses for God-knows-what-all. He followed him west on 89 and then north to Holstein. He kept me informed by cell phone, so I wasn't too far away when Samson stopped at Holstein."

"But from the air, don't all cars look alike? How did Cavers know he was following the right car?"

"If you were a *real* cop, Benny, you'd know that this is standard procedure. We put a tracking bug in his car while it was still here in Toronto. Your hunch about that professor, Benny, got us moving."

"Wasn't a hunch, it was more like a feeling I get at the back of my knees when I know I'm on to something."

"Oh, I wish I'd known that. I thought you had something a little more substantial."

"My knees have never let me down. And that nightmare I told you about clinched it."

"That nightmare. This case has everything. Can't you work in a Ouija board, Benny?"

"Look, Jack, you got your murderers, didn't you? You

found the professor in the house on the Whoozis River. What was it called again?"

"The Beatty Saugeen. Okay, the point is well taken. We followed your suggestion and we got lucky. If we admit your hunches and super-sensitive knees, you have to allow for Lady Luck playing a hand."

"Sure."

"But, Benny, how did you settle on that couple as the people to go after? The professor has a faultless rep at Simcoe College."

"The girl, Heather, had been wearing a lot of studs. The dishwasher at Barberian's remembered seeing them."

"But, Benny, wasn't she trying to get you to find Steve and Rosie?"

"Yeah, she wanted me to check myself out of the hospital so that I could more easily be dealt with. You see, she and Samson didn't know how much I remembered about my earlier visit to the university. They weren't sure I wasn't suddenly going to recall everything. And it was too chancy to try something at the hospital."

"Was that all?"

"No. Heather's visit to the hospital confused me. She put the idea in my head that *both* Steve and Rose were missing. That slowed me down. Then Samson said that Steve had a missing tooth. According to his wife, that tooth went missing the day he disappeared. Only someone who had seen him at the time of his abduction or afterwards would know that the tooth was missing."

"Where can *I* get hit on the head like *that*?" This was Sykes, who was looking at Anna.

I kept rolling. "Dr Samson made a similar mistake; he said Steve had been worried about what to get his little girl, Dympna, for her birthday. He didn't know I'd talked to Dympha herself on her birthday, which was many weeks after Steve disappeared. So, there *had* been some recent contact."

"So that's it?" Sykes groaned.

"You still don't know the wackiest part of this whole business!"

"What's that?" said two voices at once.

"It's my recurring nightmare. I was hit on the head by a flying suitcase in an upsetting railroad car."

"I think this is where I came in. I'm beginning to feel as though I bought your ticket." Sykes was out of beer and took it out on me.

"You see, I went with Rose Moss to question the people who knew Steve. That was before I got hit on the head. I talked to Dr Samson. He told me something that made me suspicious. I must have had my suspicions when he clubbed me from behind. They used to call him Gauche when he played football."

"If he was gauche, how did he make the team?"

"Touchdowns mostly. Lots of them. So I've been told. Gauche means left-handed as well as awkward."

"How did you begin to suspect him?"

"We may never know. His must have been the last face I saw before I was brained. Don't look at me! All we have is my recurring dream. It kept poking his name at me."

"It took you long enough to figure it out!" Sykes added.

"Yeah," added his partner, "and you kept it to yourself

until you brought it up in front of Samson and the rest of the people involved."

I muttered, "Sour grapes," under my breath, and then asked, "Was I wrong?"

"He's right," Sykes said to his partner through his teeth. "You would have laughed yourself pink if he'd told you earlier. The only time to admit to a clue like that is when the suspects have been booked for the crime," said Boyd, grinning.

"And when stronger evidence will support the unprovable." This from Anna.

"Yeah. I don't think we'll have much more trouble from the professor. He's quite tame now. Told me to tell you that if the muffler on your damned car hadn't attracted a police car, he'd never have had to park it behind the steak house," Boyd said, then continued, "You worked it all out, Benny. And you did it from the hospital. That's so amazing even I have to admit it."

"No, I'm not your complete armchair sleuth. Remember, I've had two shifts of nurses working for me around the clock. And I even went out one day."

"Well, next door to armchair, then."

"I'll accept that, Jack. Now, when am I going to get my suitcase packed, escape out of the hospital, and end up back home?"

"Wait a minute! Wait a minute!" It was Sykes. We looked at him until he caught his breath. "What about Flora McAlpine? The woman in the Dumpster with you. We checked her out, Benny. She went to high school with you in Grantham. How do you explain them apples?"

"She was in school with me? That's right; you told me. Flora McAlpine?"

"Yeah. Wiggle out of that. We ran her past history. You did time in grade nine together."

"Flora Mc—*Scotty!* Yes, I remember her now. Two heavy blond braids and glasses. Blue eyes squinting at the blackboard through thick lenses. I'd forgotten all about her." It was Flora's face that the television hostess had reminded me of. "Twin ramparts of blond hair," I said out loud.

Anna smiled, and took my hand.

"And she died coming to your rescue," said Jack. "We now have two witnesses who saw Flora, your old school-mate, watching through her apartment window. They were doing some sort of committee work. Flora suddenly turned, saying, 'But I *know* him!' and rushed out. They expected her to come right back. When she didn't, they went home. I talked to both of them this morning."

"Poor Flora! I guess that's as close as we are going to get until I get my wits back."

"Yeah, she could have seen you *before* you got clobbered and arrived at the Dumpster *after* you were inside. Samson then got rid of Flora the same way."

"Poor Flora," Anna said, and we nodded. We indulged in a few seconds of silence, watching the scraps of paper blow across the floor.

TWENTY-EIGHT

I FINALLY MET DYMPNA, Clea, and their parents, Laura and Steve Mapesbury. It was early September, as close as I can figure it, and the occasion was the wedding of Stella Seco's daughter, Rosie Moss, to a young American with a degree in business administration. The place was the lawn in the quadrangle at Simcoe College. I liked the irony of that. The ceremony had been held in a little chapel on St George Street, a couple of blocks from the Gothic-revival college. It was a well-attended affair; people from Stella's TV network were everywhere, some of them signing autographs. Someone told me that the Ontario government was represented by three ministers among the guests. The father of the bride, looking lost in the glare of celebrity-spotting, was taking photographs with a small Japanese camera. In spite of Stella's best attempts at upstaging the bride, Rosie was the undisputed star of the afternoon.

The weather cooperated beautifully and the sun failed to dry out the canapés. A breeze riffled the white tablecloths from time to time, but they were well anchored with platters of cheese and crackers. I soaked up as much sunshine as I could; it was the only bit of summer I was going to get. The speeches were unmemorable but perfect in the context. Turned out in a light seersucker suit from a couple of years ago, I allowed myself a glass of red wine and talked to several people who actually knew the happy couple. I faked my way through several conversations in which I pretended to be a friend of the bride or groom, as it took me. On the lawn, the large gathering of men in suits and women in hats and dresses, with sheeplike clouds overhead, made me quite giddy. I wasn't used to the wine; I'd been on the wagon all summer. All around me, women were slowly sinking into the well-tended turf to the length of their high heels, and as they grew shorter the men they were talking to grew steadily taller. I wasn't sure whether the fun of that observation was me or the wine.

By then, I had been out of the hospital for a few weeks and had been looking out for myself with some help from Anna and a few Grantham-based social workers, who were concerned about my reading, my physical well-being, and whether or not I could cope with making my bed and taking out the garbage. I still carried a Memory Book, but it had now shrunk to pocket-notebook size. It still kept track of my days and nights, reminded me about renewing my medication and other exciting things. In the grocery store I still sometimes mistook grapefruits for oranges, until I smelled or handled them. Since I liked and ate both, I didn't waste my money. Anna was a godsend in all of this, but she didn't simply look after me, she saw to it that I learned to look after myself. And, in fact, I was getting pretty good at it.

The saddest thing about leaving the rehab was leaving my nurse, Rhymes With. We exchanged addresses and met for coffee once. I hoped to see her from time to time on the outside, but I didn't. She was in Toronto, I was in Grantham. On a trip back to the hospital to give one of those talks about surviving, I found that she had moved on from the rehab. We were old war buddies; we'd survived the same bombardments together, hunkered down in the same dugouts. With her help I'd got my life together again. It was the sort of debt you never can repay. I felt that the thanks owing on my recall to life belonged to her.

Anna and I are closer than we ever have been. It was Anna who drove me to Toronto for the wedding. She would have come with me, but had to go to the races with her father. She promised to join me after the last race.

The most astonishing thing to happen that afternoon occurred when Stella, the mother of the bride, dressed in a rich burgundy summer dress, intended to dim the bride's white, came up to me and planted a firm, wet kiss on my lips. I was blindsided! As I began to get my wind back, Stella told me all about her knowledge of my recent hospital stay. She encumbered me with details of the anguish this knowledge had put her through.

I never could trust Stella. But that didn't mean I couldn't work with her or exchange friendly greetings. For instance, when she denied knowing Professor McAlpine, I didn't believe her. She'd used the feminine pronoun, referring to her as *she,* when I hadn't hinted at her sex. So she'd fed me information, even in the act of lying. I grinned at her and gave her a hug. Stella was still all smiles when she launched herself upon me one more time, then dived back into wedding festivities.

Having been warmed up by her mother, I stood in line to be greeted by the bride. While I waited my turn, the couple ahead of me talked about their summer vacation up north; talk of fishing and canoeing. I'd missed this summer completely, except for a few afternoons like this. From last summer, I remembered Stella's little cabin in the woods. The sudden cry of crows, the glimpses of the lake through pine and cedar. I remember walking along a track, heavy with pine needles, and the marina dock across the lake. To this memory, I added the picture of Anna in a canoe waving a paddle against the setting sun. I imagined listening to the sound of a camp breakfast snapping and sizzling on the wood fire.

Then, I was at the head of the reception line. Rosie grabbed me and hugged me while her eyes betrayed her emotion. It was like Stanley and Livingstone all over again, but with hugging.

"Hey! You shouldn't be crying today, young lady!"

"Oh, Benny, I'm just so glad to see you. *She* wouldn't let me talk to you. Are you all right?"

I laughed and, through an assortment of winks and grins, tried to indicate that I had survived intact. A wedding is no place for speaking the truth.

It must have been convincing, because she stopped crying. "It was my mother," she said, looking me in the eye. "I'm *so* sorry, Benny." Now she wiped away the tears and pressed a damp kiss on my cheek. "How can I thank you?"

"Forget it. Just tell me how your mother got you off the case."

"She packed me off to her brother in LA, where I met Hugh. You'll *love* Hugh, Benny. It never would have happened without you! I'll never forget what you did. Really, I won't."

"When did you see me last?"

"I came to the hospital once, as soon as I heard, but they wouldn't let me in."

"Before that. Did you take me to see Flora or Fiona? You know."

"No. I left you on campus. I went home with Heather. But I really did try to see you at the hospital."

"And Dr McAlpine?"

"She was a high-school friend of Mom's. She was my keeper twice over—as don and as Mom's eyes and ears. I still feel bad about her."

"You had nothing to do with her death. You weren't even there. Flora came to my rescue. She knew me from Grantham, too. How did your mom find out about me?"

"I went home after I heard about you and Flora. She could see it in my face and winkled the rest out of me. I'm sorry."

"She wields a strange power over people."

Rose thanked me again, then introduced me to her young man.

"Old family friend," I muttered at him as I made room for the next people in the reception line. As I moved away, Rose was whispering my secrets into the pink ear of her beloved.

I circled the refreshments table again and found a few canapés I'd missed on my first trip around.

It was easy to spot Steve Mapesbury and his family. His golden curls gave him away. Dympna looked six going on twenty. The baby was suckling her mother's breast, which she managed without upstaging any of the scheduled events. Somehow I knew, from our brief telephone acquaintance, that this might be in character for Laura Mapesbury. Steve had had his missing tooth restored and his face showed few signs of the painful ordeal he had suffered at the hands of his one-time friend and benefactor. I introduced myself to him on his way back from the drinks table. He had glasses of champagne for himself, Perrier for his wife and bubbly of another sort for the little girl.

"I don't think that he would have killed me," he said, after I had introduced myself. But I could see there was a particle of doubt in his mind. Samson, Heather, and a college dropout who had guarded Steve had all been charged. Steve was to appear as a Crown witness, having made a detailed confession in exchange for a suspended sentence. Mapesbury's description of being held captive in that Holstein house sounded less dramatic than the accounts Anna read to me from the papers. But there was a reserve of doubt in his voice as he told it to me.

"Gauche was my friend and mentor," he said. "He got me my job and found a way for me to get out of debt."

"He killed a teacher."

"I know. I know. Sometimes you get so close to people you can't see the harm."

"He might have killed you. It was the only permanent solution."

"We'll never know, will we? Come and meet my family."

On the way across the lawn, I thought of what it would be like to meet the people whose lives had passed so close to mine. It would be interesting to close the circle on these last few months. There might be some chord struck that would somehow resolve all the discordant echoes running around in my head. Still, I hesitated. But, at Steve's urging, I did go over and chat with them. In books, people always remember whom they are speaking to, but at weddings you simply chat. Nobody asked my name. Moreover, I was able to find a piece of wedding cake for Dympna. It had rosebuds on it. Weddings are all about our best hopes for the future; my anonymous appearance could hardly stir up unpleasant echoes of the past.

As I joined in a toast to the bride and groom, along with the rest of the wedding guests, I had a sudden glimpse of little Dympna staring at me from across the lawn. She moved back into the crowd, where I lost her. Nor was I about to pursue Stella further. Besides, I could see Anna making her beautiful way through the crowd toward me.

ACKNOWLEDGMENTS

IN THE MID-1960S there was a film called *Cat Ballou* starring a young Jane Fonda. In it the veteran star Lee Marvin plays the part of a dissolute former gunfighter named Kid Shaleen, a washed-up, drunken wreck, scarcely able to stand. Looking him in the face, an old-timer says to him, "Your eyes look *terrible!*" Kid Shaleen replies, "You should see them from *this* side."

In writing this book, after my illness of a couple of years ago, I've tried to show what the changes in perceptions and cognition are like as seen from "this side."

In order to bring it off, I've had a lot of help from many people. It's only fair for me to mention the names that come to mind while I still have a toehold on my memory. Those who helped to bring me and this text to this point are Beverley Slopen, Madeline Grant, Mary Adachi, Michelle Cohen, Cynthia Good, Nancy Vichert, Griff Cunningham, Don Summerhayes, Jennifer Glossop and my children, William, Charlotte, and Jacob.

AFTERWORD

BY OLIVER SACKS, MD

IN JANUARY OF 2002, I found myself thinking about the problem of alexia, an inability to read resulting from damage to a particular area in the occipital cortex, the visual part of the brain. I had been seeing a patient, an eminent pianist, who had become unable to read music, and then to read words. She saw them as clearly as ever, but now they had become "unintelligible ... meaningless ... just marks on paper." All this, my patient had explained to me in a letter, for she was perfectly able to write, though, of course, unable to read what she had written.

Shortly after this, by coincidence (such coincidences seem to happen oddly frequently in my life), I received a letter from the Canadian novelist Howard Engel, and soon afterward I met him.

One morning, some months before, he told me, he had got up feeling fine, with no sense that anything was amiss. He dressed, made breakfast, and then went out to get his newspaper. But *The Globe and Mail,* while it had the same format as always, seemed to have undergone an uncanny transformation, and had apparently been printed in "Serbo-Croatian" this morning. ("Whatever I'm looking at," he wrote to me in January of 2002, "turns into unfamiliar blocks of type that could at first glance be taken for Serbo-Croatian.") There came to his mind, in this moment, the memory of an odd case history he had read a few years earlier, my own "Case of the Colorblind Painter." He remembered in particular how my patient, Mr. I., following a traffic accident, had found himself unable to read the police accident report—how he saw print of different sizes and types, but could make nothing of it, and said it looked like "Greek" or "Hebrew" to him. Engel wondered if he, like the painter, had developed alexia, and perhaps had had, without realizing it, a stroke.

He went to the local emergency room, accompanied by his son, and the journey there seemed somewhat strange to him—roads, landmarks, the geography of Toronto, which he had known intimately for years, did not seem as immediately familiar and recognizable as usual. He was admitted to hospital, where it was ascertained with various tests that he had indeed had a small stroke, affecting only a limited area of the visual parts of the brain, the occipital cortex, on the left side. It became apparent, with further testing, that there were also some visual problems besides the alexia: a quarter of the visual field was missing, high up on the opposite side (neurologists call this a quadrantonopia), and there were some difficulties in recognition of shapes and colours, though these were mild compared to the impossibility of recognizing words or individual letters or numbers by sight.

Alexia, or "word-blindness," as it was originally called, has been recognized by neurologists since the late nineteenth century, and has always been a source of fascination, for one thinks of reading and writing as going together, and it seems bizarre, counterintuitive, that someone should be able to write but be quite unable to read what they have just written. This *alexia sine agraphia* is a classic example of what neurologists call a dissociation, or a disconnection syndrome. It has often been observed that this is a purely visual problem; people with alexia have no difficulty, for instance, recognizing letters or words if they are traced on the hand. The intactness of such tactile reading, as well as of speech recognition, showed that Engel did not have *aphasia*—a disturbance of language in general—but a pure word blindness, the result of certain areas of the visual cortex being cut off, by the stroke, from the language areas on the same side of the brain.

Thus, though he could see letters perfectly well, he could not interpret them. We normally think of reading as seamless, occurring in a single indivisible act, and one has to encounter a disconnection, such as Engel now had, to realize that, in fact, reading involves at least two, and perhaps several, separate processes and stages.

It was a huge relief for Engel to realize that, though he could not read, his ability to *write* was unimpaired—even though he might not be able to read what he had written. As an omnivorous reader, accustomed to reading newspapers each morning and a dozen or more books a week, and a prolific writer, he started to wonder what *alexia* would mean for him—how (if it failed to improve with time) it would affect his life in general, and, in particular, his life and work as a writer. For while his other symptoms—the field defects, the problems with colours and shapes—seemed to be gradually diminishing, the alexia remained unchanged. Hopefully, with time, this too would disappear.

Being able to write, without the ability to read what he had written, might be all right for a short letter or memorandum, a poem, an essay, a page or two—but how could he hope to go back to his previous work, to write a whole book, an elaborate story of crime and detection, to do all the corrections and revisions and redrafting a writer must do, without being able to read? He would have to get others to read for him, or perhaps get one of the ingenious new software programs that would allow him to scan what he had written and hear it read back to him by a computer. But either of these would still involve a radical shift, from the visuality of reading, the sight of words on a page, to an essentially auditory mode of perception and thought. Would this be possible?

These were not thoughts that came to him during his two weeks in hospital, for he was quite ill at the time and retained little memory of this period. It was when he moved to a rehabilitation hospital, where he was to spend the next six weeks, that he studied himself, what he could and could not do, and, with his therapists, explored new—sometimes radically new—ways of trying to read and to spell (which he also discovered, at this point, was very difficult for him). For the alexia affected his visual imagery as well. He could not "see" words *as* words in his mind's eye any more than he could perceive them as words when they were printed before him. Lacking this internal imagery, he had to employ other strategies for spelling. The simplest of these, he found (since his writing remained unimpaired), was to write a word in the air with his finger.

Sometimes, if he looked at a word, a couple of letters would suddenly jump out at him and be recognized—for example, the *bi* in the middle of his editor's name, though the letters before and after this remained unintelligible. (Thus guessing, inference, became supremely important.) He wondered whether such "chunking" was the way he had originally learned to read as a child, the way, perhaps, we all learn to read, even though later we may take in words as a whole. Normally the perception of letter clusters, syllables, or words, as well as inferences and hypotheses based on such perceptions, are instantaneous and automatic, so that we read fluently and swiftly, able to attend to the meaning (and perhaps the beauty) of written language, unconscious of the innumerable cues and inferences that make this possible. But it was very different for Engel at this point, for it was only occasionally that a recognizable fragment of a word might jump out, and such a fragment would be surrounded by an entire page of "Serbo-Croatian."

With help from his therapists, Engel learned to slowly and laboriously puzzle out the names of street signs or grocery aisles, or headlines in a newspaper. This, even in the absence of normal reading, made day-to-day life possible.

Engel's weeks in the rehabilitation hospital thus proved to be a neurological revelation as to how the mind works and how seemingly automatic processes can fall apart and have to be reconstructed in other ways. It was a very rich human experience as well, and Engel, indefatigably curious, and with his novelist's eye and ear fully intact, got to know his nurses and his fellow patients, their feelings about illness, their idiosyncrasies, and the intricacies of their lives. Being a patient, experiencing and observing the whole atmosphere of hospital life, stimulated Engel's imagination, and it was at this point that the idea of a new book came to him, one in which his alter ego, Benny Cooperman, would be a patient in a hospital ward with alexia (as well as a few other neurological problems), and in which he would solve a mystery—the mystery of how he had ended up, brain-damaged in a hospital ward—without ever leaving the ward.

Once he was home, Engel moved into high gear with his writing, and the manuscript of *Memory Book* rapidly took shape. Within a few weeks, he completed the first draft, and he wrote to me at this point:

I have finished my book.... As an author, you'll know how meaningless that word finish *is. What I mean to say is that I have reached the ending for the first time. How many more times will I have to finish it before it leaves the house for the last time? From now on it will be a matter of rewriting and reworking the material.... My publisher has lent me an editor, who has marked certain parts of the manuscript for my attention.... I am able to deal with the simple problems of spelling, syntax, and repetition by taking them one at a time, orienting myself on the page by making use of paragraph breaks to show me where I am.... It remains hard to get a fix on the flow of a book working this way. I can replace divots and monkey about to my heart's content, but I wonder whether I will be able to see serious plot or design flaws in time.*

I found this letter astonishing. How was Engel able to deal with the "simple" problems of spelling, syntax, and repetition when (as he wrote in his letter) "the old casual recognition of familiar words remains occluded"? The answer, or a partial answer, he wrote, lay in concentration, deciphering words letter by letter, decoding English print as if it was hieroglyphic, doing consciously and laboriously what had been, before his stroke, unconscious, automatic, and easy. "I can make myself see that certain letter group-ings are indeed familiar words, but that comes only after I have stared at the page."

He also started to bring in other senses to comple-ment the visual. Thus he often moves his tongue, almost unconsciously, as he reads, tracing the shapes of letters on the roof of his mouth. This enables him to read a good deal faster. He is about a third of the way through *Great Expectations* now, he tells me (though it now takes him a month or more to read a book he might previously have read in an evening). The neurologist Kurt Goldstein, many years ago, described something analogous to this in a patient with alexia who showed a marked improvement in the ability to read as he used his eyes to "palpate" the shapes of letters: in effect, a visual Braille.

Engel used other, more conventional help as well. His editor read the entire book to him once he had made his corrections to the first draft, and this was crucial in helping him to fix the overall structure of the book in his memory, so that he could reorganize it, work on it, thereafter, in a radical way. He also tried an electronic reading program, but found this, for various reasons, unsatisfactory.

Some years ago I saw an eminent publisher, a very literate man, who had also, like Engel, developed visual alexia. (Unlike Engel, he had developed it slowly, in consequence of a deteriorating brain disease, a gradual atrophy of the posterior visual parts of the brain—such a slow degeneration, a so-called focal atrophy, was also present in the alexic pianist whom I later saw.) This publisher found his whole orientation changing with this. He found himself becoming an auditory rather than a visual reader and writer; he devoured books on tape, and wrote by dictation—not only letters and memoranda, but essays, and an entire memoir. Engel, by contrast, has remained much more visual, and seems to prefer the tussle of trying to read books and write them visually, despite his difficulties with this.

Engel sometimes wonders about other writers who have struggled with alexia. He tells me that H. L. Mencken lost the ability to read after he suffered a stroke, but I can ascertain no details of this—Mencken may have suffered a pure alexia, but it seems likely that he had a much more debilitating aphasic stroke, for he did not write in the ten years following his stroke. By chance, today, looking at the August 12, 2004, issue of the *New York Review of Books* which just arrived, I see a review of a book by the German novelist Gert Hofman. This and two other novels, I read, "were written after Gert Hofman suffered a stroke, which left him unable to read. He dictated them to his wife, and she read the drafts back to him 'to correct and embellish aloud.'"

The alexic pianist whom I wrote about ("The Case of Anna H."), after she became unable to read music, developed an extraordinary ability to listen to orchestral and choral works and arrange them for piano entirely in her mind, where before she would have needed manuscript paper and pencil to do this. The alexic publisher also told me that his power to "hear" what he had read or written, and to organize it in his mind, had steadily increased after his alexia. Similar compensatory heightenings are almost universal in the blind—not only the congenitally blind, but those who have lost their sight later in life—and it seems likely that it also occurs in the alexic.

Whatever the strategies employed—whether it is visually learning the shapes of letters anew, or copying and then "reading" them by means of tongue or finger movements, or developing heightened powers of auditory and conceptual memory, there seem to be many ways by which a person with alexia—especially a resourceful, verbal, highly motivated person like a writer—can get around the deficit, find new ways of doing things now that the old ways are unavailable. No doubt, too, there are changes in the brain underlying these adaptations, though these might be beyond the power of present brain imaging to show.

This is not to minimize the continuing impact of a condition like alexia in a world full of newspapers and books, maps and street signs, printed labels and directions on everything one uses—and above all, its impact on a writer like Howard Engel, and the continuing, daily struggle to transcend it, one way or another. It is a struggle that calls for heroic determination and courage, as well as great resourcefulness, patience, and, not least, humour—simply to survive, let alone to produce, as Howard Engel has done, a book (and he tells me that he has just completed another Benny Cooperman novel, to be published after *Memory Book*).

Given this struggle, this of-necessity unorthodox way of writing, does Engel succeed as a writer? Is the present volume up to the standard of the previous Benny Cooperman novels? My answer, as a reader of detective stories, is "Yes, absolutely." Indeed, I think this may be the most remarkable of them all, because of its special personal dimension. There have been a number of recent books that have incorporated medical or neurological themes (detectives with Tourette's syndrome, detectives with autism, etc.)—and indeed this goes back, in suspense novels, to the fiction of Wilkie Collins in the nineteenth century. But *Memory Book* has a unique depth and authenticity, because Howard Engel has known and traversed all that he writes about. He has, as Bertrand Russell would say, "knowledge by experience," and no knowledge by description can ever match this.